Ötzi, the Iceman

The Full Facts at a Glance

Ötzi, the Iceman

The Full Facts at a Glance

Angelika Fleckinger · Folio Vienna/Bolzano

THANKS

The following people contributed in various ways to the creation of this book:
Gilberto Artioli, Petra Augschöll, Rolf Barth, Eduard Egarter Vigl, Markus Egg, Erwin Egger, Luis Egger, Paul Gleirscher, Paul Gostner, Sonia E. Guillen, Hermann Gummerer, Irene Hager von Strobele, Kathrin Kötz, Walter Leitner, Tom Loy, Wolfgang Müller, Augustin Ochsenreiter, Klaus Oeggl, Harm Paulsen, Annaluisa Pedrotti, Alois Pirpamer, Peter Paul Pramstaller, Anne Reichert, Silvia Renhart, Marco Samadelli, Horst Seidler, Ester Solderer, Gudrun Sulzenbacher, Ivana Trocker, Margit Tumler, Silvia Quevedo – special thanks go to them all.

© Folio, Vienna/Bolzano, and the South Tyrol Museum of Archaeology, Bolzano
Third edition 2007
Translation: Geraint Williams
Graphic design and prepress: no.parking, Vicenza
Scans: Lanarepro, Lana; Typestudio, Bolzano; Typoplus, Appiano
Printing: Dipdruck, Brunico
ISBN 978-3-85256-244-5

www.folioverlag.com

CONTENTS

THE FASCINATION OF THE ICEMAN

The Iceman on display at the South Tyrol Museum of Archaeology is one of the world's best-known mummies, ranking alongside London's Lindow Man, the Tollund Man in Denmark, Juanita from Peru and the Moor Corpses of the Silkeborg Museum in Denmark. What is so unique about this particular find is that we are dealing with a man, whose life came to an abrupt end, leaving him and a large part of his clothing and possessions intact. For the first time in the history of medicine and archaeology, it has been possible to conduct anatomical studies on a corpse dating from the fourth millennium BC and to study items of Stone Age clothing and equipment in detail.

Years of research undertaken at the scene of the find using the most modern methods have provided a previously unavailable glimpse into the daily life of Stone Age man, his environment and extraordinary ability to survive in it and use its limited resources.

Although new knowledge is constantly emerging, the Iceman remains a source of further riddles.

This book will familiarize the reader with the results of research conducted by a wide range of scientific disciplines.

SÜDTIROLER ARCHÄOLOGIEMUSEUM
MUSEO ARCHEOLOGICO DELL' ALTO ADIGE
SOUTH TYROL MUSEUM OF ARCHAEOLOGY

Dr Bruno Hosp
President of the South Tyrol Provincial Museums

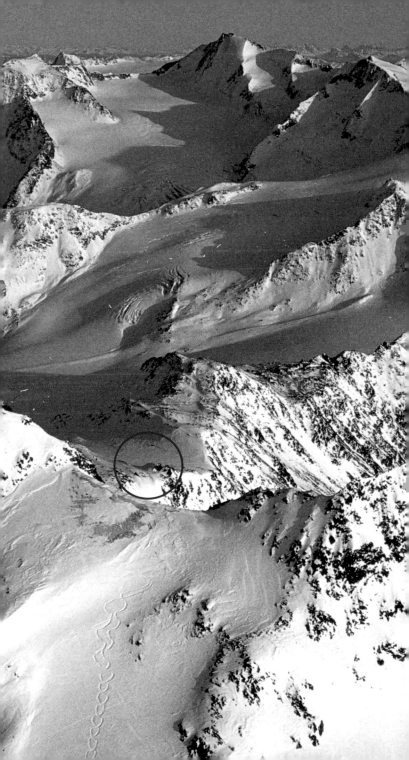

First recorded image
of the mummy

THE FIND OF THE CENTURY

The Discovery

Thursday, September 19, 1991 – 1.30pm
Ötztal Alps/Tisenjoch – 3210m above sea level (South Tyrol, Italy)

On a sunny day in late September, two hikers from Nuremberg, Germany, Erika and Helmut Simon, were walking in the Ötztal Alps. Descending from the Finail peak in the Tisenjoch area, the Simons decided to take a short cut, and moved off the marked footpath.

As they walked past a rocky gully filled with melt water, they noticed something brown on the gully bed. First they took it to

be some sort of refuse but on closer inspection they realized they had come across a human corpse. Only the back of the head, the bare shoulders and part of his back jutted out of the ice and melt water. The corpse's chest lay against a flat rock with its face obscured. Beside the corpse the two hikers noticed pieces of rolled up birch bark.

The discoverers

Before leaving the scene, they took a photograph of what they thought to be the unfortunate victim of a mountaineering accident from a few years back.

An hour later, the Simons reached the Similaun mountain refuge and informed the landlord, Markus Pirpamer, of their discovery. As the scene of the find lies along the Italian-Austrian border, Pirpamer decided to alert both the Italian carabinieri in Schnals and the Austrian gendarmes in Sölden. Later that day, Pirpamer and one of his employees visited the site and discovered various objects in the vicinity of the corpse such as pieces of wood, lengths of string, clumps of hair and strips of hide. These they picked up, inspected and put back in their place.

At this point in time nobody could have imagined that the dead man and these objects were soon to become famous throughout the world. The story of the archaeological sensation of the twentieth century had just begun.

The First Recovery Attempt

Friday, September 20, 1991

The day after the discovery of the corpse, an Austrian team initiated the first attempt to remove the man from the ice. By then the weather had got considerably worse. Using a pneumatic drill, the gendarme Anton Koler and mountain refuge landlord Markus Pirpamer tried to free the corpse. Due to the constant flow of melt water, the two men were obliged to work virtually under water, causing damage to the corpse's left hip. After half an hour, with the body partially free, the drill ran out of fuel. With the weather worsening by the minute and, lacking the necessary tools, the team were forced to abandon their work.

Koler removed the axe with the right-angled shaft, which lay on the edge of the gully and took it to the gendarmerie post in Sölden. This understandably caused a sensation among the many by-standers who had already made it to the scene but nobody realised that this 'curious pickaxe' was actually of pre-historic origin.

Rumours spread to the effect that the corpse displayed burns and a head wound and that it had even been tied up. This finally led to the opening of a criminal enquiry into the man's identity and the possible involvement of a third party. This enquiry was filed by the Public Prosecutor under the number ST 13 UT 6407/91. Criminal proceedings were opened against an unidentified suspect. It all seemed perfectly routine, but then again, no one could have guessed the sheer age of the dead man.

Further finds: an unsightly collection of various materials

Saturday, September 21, 1991

On the following day, attempts at recovering the corpse were again hindered – this time due to the fact that no helicopters were available. Acting on official orders, Pirpamer and his employee were asked to go to the scene and cover the corpse with a plastic bag to protect it from the usual crowds of weekend hikers.

That day the world-famous mountaineers Hans Kammerlander and Reinhold Messner reached the Similaun refuge while on a tour of the South Tyrol. With the bar of the refuge already buzzing with heated discussions, the two mountaineers could not contain their curiosity and decided to take a look for themselves.

They observed the first details of the dead man's clothing: the finely sewn leather leggings, the shoes and the grass matting. In order to examine the corpse more closely, they attempted to free it from the ice, Messner using a ski stick and Kammerlander a piece of wood which turned out to be a piece of the Iceman's backpack frame.

Also present was Kurt Fritz, a mountain guide, who lifted the dead man's head to reveal his face for the first time. Further searches threw up other objects such as the remains of birch-bark receptacles, a longbow leaning against the wall of the gully and a wooden backpack frame. From memory Markus Pirpamer sketched the axe found on the previous day and Messner estimated the finds to be at least 500 years old, perhaps even as much as 3,000 years old. Oddly enough, a journalist urged him not to put their age at any more than 500 years old.

Sunday, September 22, 1991

On the Sunday Alois Pirpamer, head of the local mountain rescue, made his way to the Tisenjoch in the company of Franz Gurschler. Their aim was to prepare the corpse for its recovery the following day. After chipping the corpse free with ice picks, they collected the surrounding objects and put them in a plastic rubbish bag. The very same day, Pirpamer returned to his hotel in Vent with the bag over his shoulder.

Grotesque Grip

Alois Pirpamer, Head of Mountain Rescue, 'at first Franz Gurschler and I were unable to remove the right hand from the ice, as it seemed to be trapped between two rocks. By twisting the forearm, we finally managed to free the hand and noticed that the dead man was holding something. Later it turned out to be a dagger.'

The Recovery

Monday, September 23, 1991 – 12.37 pm

On the Monday the corpse could finally be extracted from the ice. In the meantime, newspaper articles on the find had already appeared.

Around midday a helicopter with a TV crew from Austrian National Television reached the Tisenjoch. Snow had fallen over night and due to the extremely low temperatures, the corpse was once again frozen solid into the ice. Under the leadership of Rainer Henn of the Innsbruck University Institute of Forensic Medicine, the recovery took place with cameras running. As no archaeologist had yet been present, the filmed footage proved to be an important document for the scientific community.

Using ice picks and ski poles, the mummy was fully extracted from the ice. From the melt water emerged numerous pieces of leather and hide, string, straps and clumps of hay, which were placed in a pile beside the corpse. Among the finds was a dagger with a flint blade and wooden handle. In the first television interviews, the forensic doctor Henn spoke very cautiously about the corpse's possible age but he did state that this was not a typical glacier mummy displaying the signs of adipocere – a waxy substance that grows on dead bodies – that he knew from previous experience.

The corpse was packed into a body bag along with the latest finds. With the lower section of the longbow still frozen into the

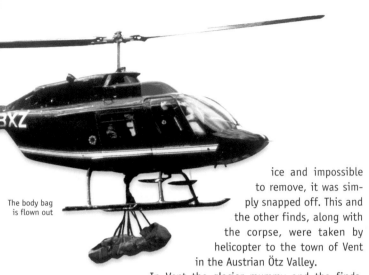

The body bag
is flown out

ice and impossible to remove, it was simply snapped off. This and the other finds, along with the corpse, were taken by helicopter to the town of Vent in the Austrian Ötz Valley.

In Vent the glacier mummy and the finds, together with those collected by Alois Pirpamer on the previous day and the axe earlier taken to the gendarmerie post in Sölden, were placed in a wooden coffin. In the opinion of those present, the corpse was already becoming the focus of disagreeable rumours. The public prosecutor ordered the corpse to be taken by hearse to the Institute for Forensic Medicine in Innsbruck.

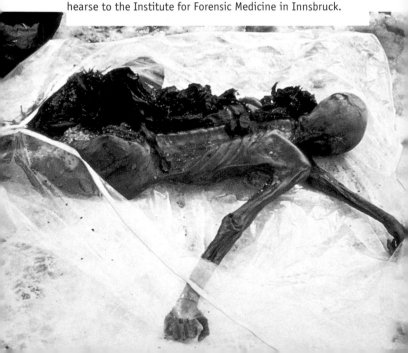

Incredible News

Tuesday, September 24, 1991

The following Tuesday morning an archaeologist was finally brought in. Professor of Ancient and Early History at the University of Innsbruck, Konrad Spindler inspected the corpse and the finds and, based on the typology of the axe, immediately dated the whole find to be 'at least four thousand years old'. Clearly the man must have lived in the Early Bronze Age at the very latest.

Until this discovery, such a well preserved, several thousand year old find of a human in complete clothing with numerous personal belongings had never been seen anywhere in the world. In the meantime, the mummy was thawed out at a temperature of 18°C. To prevent its decomposition, unprecedented conservation measures had to be taken. It was clear from the start that the body could only be conserved by artificially creating the same conditions which had preserved the corpse over thousands of years. The mummy was stored in a cold cell at a temperature of −6°C. In order to obtain conditions of maximum air humidity, the corpse was wrapped in a sterile operating gown and covered with various layers of crushed ice made of sterilized water. In this way it was possible to simulate the natural conditions of the glacier where 100% air humidity is the norm.

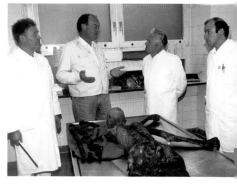

Prof. Konrad Spindler (second from left) was the first to realise the importance of the find.

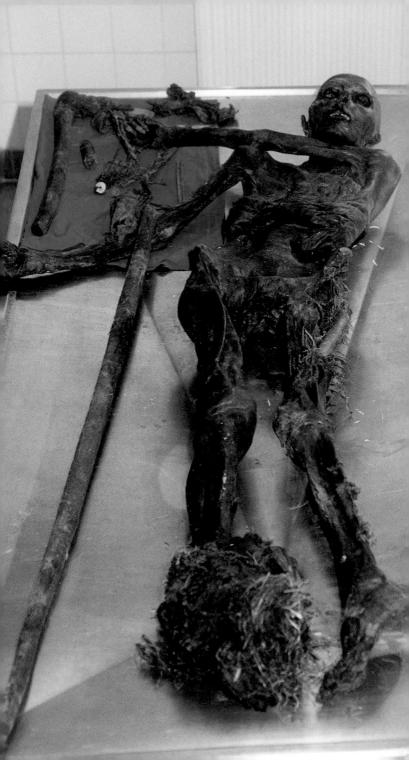

No Further Doubts...

At least 4,000 to 5,000 years old. This unbelievable discovery immediately hit the headlines and set the Iceman's unprecedented media career in motion. Journalists from all over the world besieged scientists, attempted to decipher details and speculate wildly as to the circumstances of the Iceman's life and death. What began as a momentous archaeological event quickly became known as the find of the century and a sensation of the first order.

One journalist even alleged that the whole thing was an elaborate fraud. A hoaxer, possibly even one of the scientists themselves, had planted an Egyptian or Peruvian mummy at the scene of the find. His theory was based on the lack of adipocere, which is so common in glacier mummies, and the absence of genitals. Unlike in Egypt, castration was never a traditional practice in the Alps. Later research showed however that the Iceman's genitalia were actually completely intact.

☞ Heim, M./Nosko, W.: Die Ötztal-Fälschung − Anatomie einer archäologischen Groteske. Reinbeck 1993.

The C-14 Method (Radio Carbon Dating)

The Carbon-14 method is the best known means of dating organic material and was developed by W.F. Libby in 1946−47. The tissue of every living being absorbs the C-14 isotopes in the atmosphere. On death, the flow of C-14 is interrupted and gradually disappears, with only half remaining after 5,730 years. The amount of C-14 isotopes still present in organic matter can be measured using a mass spectrometer and the time of death of a living being thus calculated.

---

tzi and the other finds − with his right shoe
till on his foot − on the operating table

Undisputable proof of the authenticity and extraordinary age of the Iceman and his possessions was provided by C-14 analysis. Tissue samples from the corpse and the finds were analysed at four different scientific institutions and the results were unanimous: the Iceman lived between 3350 and 3100 BC.

The Iceman was therefore alive some 5,000 years ago, at a time when the discovery of copper was revolutionizing the simple agricultural and cattle-breeding lifestyle of European man.

The World 5,000 Years ago

The Iceman had already been buried in the glacier for 600 years when the Egyptian pharaoh Cheops ordered the building of the pyramid that bore his name (circa 2550 BC). Stonehenge in England only dates from a few hundred years after the glacier mummy's death. The first advanced European civilization developed on Crete around 2300 BC. The Minoan Palaces of Knossos and Phaistos with their magnificent frescoes are splendid testimonies to the cultural life of this kingdom. The Minoan culture was influenced both by the advances of Egypt and Asia Minor – as early as 3100 BC, Mesopotamia, on the plain between the Tigris and the Euphrates, was home to cities with thousands of inhabitants and an extraordinary irrigation system had converted the land into a fertile plain. The inhabitants of these first cities were Sumerians. They also developed their own alphabet.

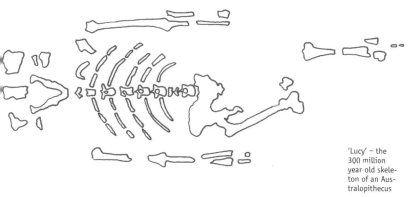

'Lucy' – the 300 million year-old skeleton of an Australopithecus

THE MUMMY – A SENSATIONAL DISCOVERY

Naming him?

Naming the glacier mummy immediately posed a number of problems. Archaeological finds should be named after their geographical location as described on official maps. The nearest marked geographical location to the find is the Hauslabjoch, a peak 330 m away. Topographically the Tisenjoch peak lies far nearer but does not appear on any official map. While the authorities grappled with the problem of finding an official denomination, the search for a popular name produced numerous examples in the press. In addition to relatively objective names such as 'The Man from Hauslabjoch', 'The Man from Tisenjoch', 'Similaun Man', 'Homo tirolensis' and 'The Man in the Ice', journalists came up with a wide variety of nicknames, some of which were bizarre to say the least.

Journalist Karl Wendl was the first to coin the name 'Ötzi' (pronounced 'urtzee'), in reference to the adjoining Ötz Valley, in an article for the Viennese *Arbeiter-Zeitung* on September 26, 1991. According to a resolution by the South Tyrol Provincial Government on July 2, 1997, the official name for the glacier mummy is 'Der Mann aus dem Eis'/'L'Uomo venuto dal ghiaccio'/'The Iceman'.

'Ötzi'

'This dried out, grotesque corpse must be made more positive, more loveable, if it is to be turned into a good story', remarked the journalist Karl Wendl.

The practice of attributing human finds with diminutives or nicknames is extremely rare. However, when the 3,2 million-year-old skeleton of an Australopithecus was discovered in Ethiopia in 1976, she was baptized 'Lucy' after the Beatles' song 'Lucy In The Sky With Diamonds'. In 1995, the mummy of an Inca girl sacrificed to the gods 500 years earlier was found on the side of the Ampato volcano in Peru. The official name 'Ice Maiden' was quickly converted to 'Juanita'.

By giving the dead a popular name, their strange, corpse-like nature disappears, making them life-like in people's minds. The glacier mummy was also rendered 'media friendly' by the use of nicknames.

☞ Ortner, L.: Von der Gletscherleiche zu unserem Urahnl Ötzi.
Zur Benennungspraxis in der Presse.
In: Deutsche Sprache 2/1993, pp. 97–127.

Juanita

BURIED BENEATH THE GLACIER

The Scene of the Find

The Iceman was discovered in a 40 m-long, 2.5–3 m-deep and 5–8 m-wide rocky gully, surrounded by steep stonewalls at a height of 3,210 m above sea level. This location, just off the path between the Similaun refuge and the Tisenjoch peak, protected the man and his possessions from the extraordinary power of the ice, which, over the years, covered the gully.

Even as late as 1922, when the border between Austria and Italy was newly demarcated, a 20 m-deep layer of snow covered this currently ice-free area. In 1991, the melting process had advanced considerably due to the unusually warm summer of the previous year. It was only in the bed of the gully that a 60–80 cm layer of ice remained. The melting of the glacier was accelerated that year by a layer of sand blown over from the Sahara that had dyed the snow and ice fields a yellowish brown colour. In fact it had shrunk to its lowest level in thousands of years to reveal what had long been buried there.

When the man in the rocky gully died, it was in all probability free of snow and ice.

This is the rocky gully where the mummy was discovered.

The Border Question

Soon after the recovery of the mummy, rumours spread that the dead man had actually been found on the Italian side of the border, not in Austria as originally thought.

The border between the two countries was redrawn along the watershed of the Inn and Etsch Valleys after the First World War in 1919, in accordance with the Treaty of St. Germain. In the area of the Tisenjoch, the exact location of the watershed was difficult to establish at that time due to the presence of the glacier. A newly ordered survey of the border was carried out on October 2, 1991. First of all it was necessary to find the boundary stones laid along this mountainous stretch after the First World War to mark out the border and then to trace the borderline using a theodolite and a distance-measuring instrument. This new survey was then compared with the original frontier documents and found to be extraordinarily accurate. The next step was to relate the exact spot where the Iceman was found, marked by a cross, to a baseline formed by two of the boundary stones using a distance-measuring instrument. The new border survey clearly showed that the site of the find is 92.56 m beyond the frontier in the South Tyrol i.e. in Italy.

Even if the site of the find drains towards the Inn Valley i.e. to the north, the boundary established after the First World War remains valid under international law. The province of South Tyrol therefore claimed property rights but entrusted the finds as a whole to the University of Innsbruck until scientific examinations were completed. The South Tyrolean authorities also gave permission for the Institute for Primeval and Early History of the University of Innsbruck to initiate further archaeological investigation on the site.

A Memorial

Today a four-metre-high stone pyramid marks the spot where the glacier mummy was discovered.

☞ Neubauer, M.: Ötzi und die Staatsgrenze. Bericht über die Arbeiten zur Feststellung der Fundstelle in Bezug auf die Staatsgrenze Österreich–Italien am Hauslabjoch. In: EVM. Eich- u. Vermessungsmagazin, Wien 67/1992, pp. 5–11.

Was the mummy ever exposed before its discovery?

According to Klaus Oeggl of the Botanical Institute of the University of Innsbruck, 'in my opinion the scenario was as follows: the Iceman died on the Tisenjoch in spring. According to the climatic conditions prevalent in this high mountain area, snow still lay on the ground at this time of the year. During the following summer, the snow melted and the body and the rest of the finds lay in the melt water, with the result that the wooden objects were displaced, the body turned through 90° and its skin peeled off. When the melt water drained off at the end of the summer, mummification by means of dehydration followed. Finally the finds were covered in snow and later embedded in the ice. Paleoclimatic data for the Eastern Alps indicates that this could not have been the only instance when the contents of the gully were thawed out. Other periods of warm weather have been recorded for the second half of the third century BC and during Roman times (first to fourth century AD).

The site of the find beside the Italian-Austrian border

Border survey

Archaeologists sift through the mud like gold prospectors.

Excavations into the Ice

On Wednesday, September 25, six days after the sensational discovery, glacier experts from the Institute of High Mountain Research set out for the Hauslabjoch. There, on the edge of the scene of the find in a crack in the rock, they discovered a fully intact quiver with its contents. After carefully extracting it from the ice, they took it back to Innsbruck. This, however, was only one of a number of spectacular finds that would be unearthed during the archaeological investigation.

The first actual archaeological examination of the gully took place between October 3 and 5, 1991. Its aim was to document the exact position of the mummy and the rest of the finds in the form of a detailed contour plan. It was the first time an archaeological excavation had had to be undertaken on a glacier.

This revealed various remains of hide and leather as well as pieces of a net made of grass string and the remains of a birch-bark container and its contents. On the flat stone slab where the dead man lay, sections of grass matting emerged. However, the onset of winter put an end to further archaeological investigation that year.

Between July 20 and August 25, 1992, a second archaeological examination was carried out by various institutes under the direction of the Ancient Monuments Office of the Autonomous Province of Bolzano. Although long periods of fine weather in 1992 had melted much of the snow, large quantities still had to be shovelled away before the work of the specialists could begin. The ice in the crevices and between blocks of stone had to be melted using steam-blowers and driers. The work was also complicated by the fact that melt water descending from a snowfield higher up constantly flooded the gully. This water had to be pumped out and sieved several times over. From this sediment came numerous small finds – further pieces of the Iceman's kit such as leather and hide remnants, grasses and string but also pieces of skin, muscle fibres, hair and a fingernail. The section of the broken longbow that had been stuck fast in the ice the year before could finally be extracted. Around the stone slab where the Iceman had lain, his excellently preserved bearskin cap was discovered.

In both investigations the contents of the rocky gully were exhaustively examined.

Archaeological excavations in the glacier ice

Where was Ötzi's kit found?

The Iceman's equipment was carefully laid out before his death. This can be seen from the position of his quiver, discovered four metres away from the man on a flat stone in the northwest corner of the gully. The longbow, axe and backpack lay on the southwest side of the gully. When the longbow was discovered, it was still leaning against the stonewall. The melt water had shifted the rest of his kit to the edges of the gully, in the immediate vicinity of the dead man.

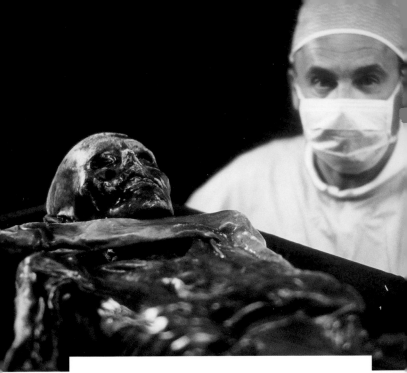

A MUMMY AS A PATIENT

The uniqueness of the Iceman has not only interested archaeologists – for the first time researchers from the most diverse areas of the natural sciences have had the opportunity to examine a 5,000-year-old damp mummy.

All over the world research teams and scientific institutions have been and are working on various aspects of Ötzi's life. Using modern visual techniques, anatomical idiosyncrasies and pathological alterations have been diagnosed. Often new experimental techniques had to be developed in order to carry out these examinations. In this way it was possible to examine individual items that could not normally be studied on human remains from prehistoric times.

Today, a board of experts assembled by the South Tyrol Museum of Archaeology made up of anthropologists and physicians coordinates research on the Iceman. There are still around 30 reports published annually by research teams the world over as examination methods are in a constant state of development, with new issues regularly coming to light.

What did Ötzi look like?

In basic terms, the physiognomy of the Iceman does not differ substantially from that of human beings today.

During the process of mummification, the mummy shrank and today measures 1.54 m. It was calculated that during his lifetime, his height must have been around 1.60 m. His shoe size is a continental 38. Ötzi therefore displays the average body measurements of the Neolithic population. His eyeballs have dried out and remain in the sockets, clearly showing that his iris was blue.

The Iceman has very little subcutaneous fat tissue, in fact no excess fat at all on his body, and must have weighed around 50 kg. The mummified body today weighs some 13 kg.

Being the mummy of a man, rumours in the sensationalist press abounded to the effect that his genitals were missing, that they had been 'lost' during the recovery. The official anatomical examination found, however, that the Iceman's genital area was free of anomalies.

The reconstruction
of the Iceman

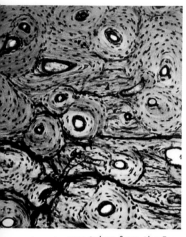

A sample of Ötzi's bone tissue

How old was the Iceman?

In adults it is difficult to ascertain their exact age at the time of death since the process of growth has already come to an end.

In order to calculate the age of the Iceman, his bone structure was put under the microscope. Due to the continual transformation of the bone tissue, characteristic changes occur in the bone structure as a person ages. A small cylinder-shaped sample of bone was taken from the Iceman's upper femur. During the histological study, the number of osteone in the bone were counted. The surface area was also measured and together, these two parameters relate directly to a person's age. The average reading from a total of nine samples resulted in an age of 45.7 years, with a margin of error of plus or minus five years. By Late Stone Age standards, the Iceman had lived to a relatively old age.

Ötzi's Hair

At the time of his discovery, the Iceman was almost completely bald. One of the most sensitive organs in the human body is the epidermis. On death, its structure alters rapidly with the process of decomposition that can lead to loss of hair. The numerous clumps of hair discovered at the scene of the find were both animal and human body hair, as the Bundeskriminalamt in Wiesbaden and the German Wool Research Institute of Aachen demonstrated.

One lock of hair is made up of several hundred strands and proves that the Iceman had a head of wavy, dark brown to black hair over nine centimetres long. The hair structure indicates that Ötzi wore his hair loose and did not plait it. It is highly probable that he also had a beard due to the large number of short, thick hairs found at the site. Other hair remains were identified as coming from his armpits, pubic area and other parts of his body.

When Ötzi's hair was analysed for traces of metal, the results showed considerably lower levels of lead than in people today. On the other hand, the arsenic content was much higher. In all probability the Iceman occasionally worked with minerals, probably copper smelting.

 Witting, M./Wortmann, G.: Untersuchungen an Haaren aus den Begleitfunden des Eismannes vom Hauslabjoch. In: Höpfel, Frank et al.: Der Mann im Eis. Band 1. Innsbruck 1992, pp. 273–297.

Little Irritations...

The oldest deer louse ever found was among the animal hairs in the Iceman's possessions. Deer lice are ectoparasites and bloodsuckers present on the bodies of wild animals but they also occasionally turn up on human beings.

Despite a thorough examination of Ötzi's hair, no lice were found. However, two human fleas were discovered in his clothing.

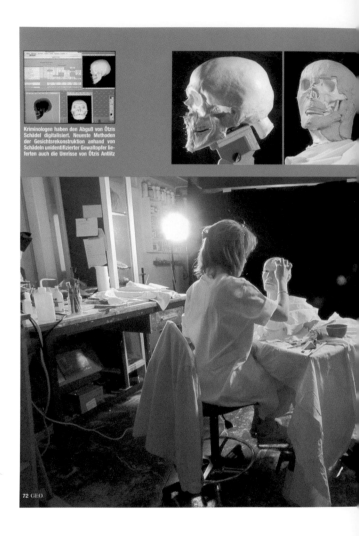

Kriminologen haben den Abguß von Ötzis Schädel digitalisiert. Neueste Methoden der Gesichtsrekonstruktion anhand von Schädeln unidentifizierter Gewaltopfer lieferten auch die Umrisse von Ötzis Antlitz

72 GEO

The Search for Ötzi's Face

Due to the time he spent beneath the ice, Ötzi's face was considerably deformed. However, it is still possible to get a picture of the way he really looked.

Shortly after the discovery, a criminologist from Vienna produced identikit pictures of the Iceman using a reconstruction method developed by the FBI. The American Palaeolithic artist John Gurche, creator of the dinosaur models for 'Jurassic Park', was

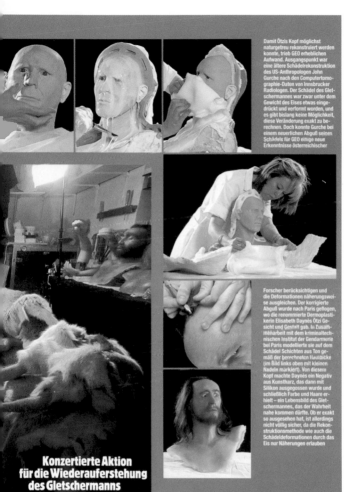

Damit Ötzis Kopf möglichst naturgetreu rekonstruiert werden konnte, trieb GEO erheblichen Aufwand. Ausgangspunkt war eine ältere Schädelrekonstruktion des US-Anthropologen John Gurche nach den Computertomographie-Daten von Innsbrucker Radiologen. Der Schädel des Gletschermannes war zwar unter dem Gewicht des Eises etwas eingedrückt und verformt worden, und es gibt bislang keine Möglichkeit, diese Veränderung exakt zu berechnen. Doch konnte Gurche bei einem neuerlichen Abguß seines Schädels für GEO einige neue Erkenntnisse österreichischer

Forscher berücksichtigen und die Deformationen näherungsweise ausgleichen. Der korrigierte Abguß wurde nach Paris geflogen, wo die renommierte Dermoplastikerin Elisabeth Daynès Ötzi Gesicht und Gestalt gab. In Zusammenarbeit mit dem kriminaltechnischen Institut der Gendarmerie bei Paris modellierte sie auf dem Schädel Schichten aus Ton gemäß der berechneten Hautdicke (im Bild links oben mit kleinen Nadeln markiert). Von diesem Kopf machte Daynès ein Negativ aus Kunstharz, das dann mit Silikon ausgegossen wurde und schließlich Farbe und Haare erhielt – ein Lebensbild des Gletschermannes, das der Wahrheit nahe kommen dürfte. Ob er exakt so ausgesehen hat, ist allerdings nicht völlig sicher, da die Rekonstruktionsmethode wie auch die Schädeldeformationen durch das Eis nur Näherungen erlauben

Konzertierte Aktion für die Wiederauferstehung des Gletschermanns

The travel magazine GEO shows how Ötzi's face was reconstructed as faithfully as possible.

☞ Ötzi. Der Mann aus der Steinzeit. In: GEO 10/1996, pp. 72 f.

the first to attempt a reconstruction of Ötzi's face in the form of a model. The plastic surgeon Elisabeth Daynès worked together with the Criminal Technical Institute of the Parisian Gendarmerie on a second soft reconstruction. The Scottish forensic scientist Peter Vanezis created the facial reconstruction on display at the South Tyrol Museum of Archaeology.

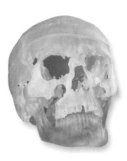

The Reconstruction of the Skull

A three-dimensional image of the skull's soft- and bone structure

A stereolithographic model of the skull

A plastic reconstruction of the skull using a spiral computed tomogram

The computer tomography images produced during the course of the various scientific examinations formed the basis for the three-dimensional reconstruction of the Iceman's skeleton. Using stereo lithography, it was possible to convert the CT readings into a three-dimensional model. These experiments used computer-steered technology in which an extremely accurate ultra-violet laser covers each anatomical detail with a layer of acrylic resin. In this way, a model of the skull could be fashioned in the space of some 40 hours, corresponding exactly to the original. By examining this model, it became clear that the effects of the pressure of ice had deformed the skull in several places.

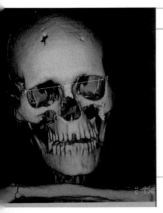

Space Age Technology

Before the discovery of the Iceman, stereo lithography had only been employed in space exploration and the car industry, so for the first time this technique was used on a human being. Since then it has been successfully incorporated into medical science. In complex neurological operations, incisions can be traced in advance using 3-D models.

The State of Ötzi's Health

Having lived to the age of 45, Ötzi must surely have been among the eldest members of his community. And his body displays clear signs of degeneration – his joints are worn and his arteries hardened. The Iceman's twelfth pair of ribs is also missing but this rare anomaly did not in any way hinder his activities.

Ötzi's body also displays signs of injuries that he must have sustained during his lifetime. He is seen to have a well healed multiple rib fracture on the left of the thorax as well as a fracture of his nasal bone. A cyst-like growth on the little toe of his left foot may well have been caused by frostbite.

Stone Age Stress?

Examinations of the fingernail found during the second archaeological excavation reveal that he suffered from a chronic illness of some kind. Three so-called Beau-Reil lines across the nail indicate that Ötzi's immune system was subjected to periods of severe stress eight, 13 and 16 weeks before his death. The most recent line is also the most pronounced.

Teeth

At first sight, the Iceman has a remarkable diastema between the two incisors on his upper jaw. This four-millimetre gap is an abnormality that is frequently inherited. Another peculiarity is his lack of wisdom teeth, an increasingly familiar feature today given the evolutionary trend towards smaller jawbones.

Particularly noticeable is the extent to which his teeth are worn down. The crown of one of his incisors has been reduced by up to three millimetres! This must have been caused by the consumption of stone-ground wheat containing grit. His teeth are however entirely free of caries.

The left-hand side of his upper jaw shows signs of considerable wear, probably due to the fact that Ötzi often used his teeth as 'tools' for working with wood, bones, leather and sinews.

Stone Age Chewing Gum?

During excavations of Neolithic pile dwellings beside Lake Constance, lumps of birch tar were discovered which displayed clear signs of having been chewed. It is still unclear whether birch tar was 'consumed' in Prehistoric times or just used as glue.

Stored between his teeth...

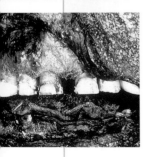

According to Dr Wolfgang Müller of the Research School of Earth Sciences of the Australian National University, 'By examining a sample of the mummy's dental enamel weighing only a few milligrams for its isotopic composition, I was able to ascertain where the Iceman had spent his early childhood. The strontium, lead and oxygen isotopes stored in human dental enamel reflect the food, soil and water composition of a person's precise habitat. Up to now, we are sure that he spent his childhood in an area of lime-rich soils. Our future detective work will attempt to make a more accurate classification by analysing soil samples.'

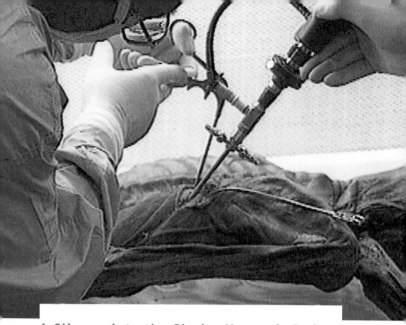

Endoscopic examination (Screenshot)

A Glimpse into the Glacier Mummy's Body

The endoscopic examination of the mummy was one of the greatest challenges facing the medical research programme. For these micro-surgical interventions, specially designed precision instruments made of titanium had to be developed in order to avoid contaminating tissue samples with heavy metals. Samples from the internal organs were obtained by cutting an aperture in the mummy's back. Using computers, the instruments could be steered to exact points where samples were to be taken. This intervention was filmed using a special high-definition camera.

This glimpse inside the mummy's body confirmed that some of the mummy's organs had shrunk considerably and moved from their usual positions. The Iceman's lungs are blackened and show the presence of soot particles, probably the result of spending so much time in front of open fires.

The tissue samples taken endoscopically were and will be further analysed by scientists and institutions from all over the world.

This virtual journey through Ötzi's body can be seen on video at the South Tyrol Archaeology Museum.

A view of his smoke blackened lungs

DNA Analysis

The original mitochondrial DNA examination proved that the Iceman lived in the Late Stone Age and that he can be classified as a member of the Central European population.

Such examinations are not only of interest to anthropologists but also to modern medicine. These results should enable doctors to ascertain whether genetically transmitted illnesses affecting ancient peoples can still be found today, or whether genetic structures have altered over time.

The DNA analysis was not limited to the Iceman's body however. DNA sequences could also be identified from the bacteria, fungi, plants and animal remains discovered at the scene of the find.

☞ Handt, O. et al.: Molecular Genetic Analyses of the Tyrolean Ice Man. In: Science 264/1994, pp. 1175–1178.

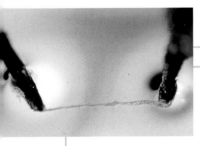

A trial of strength using Ötzi's muscle fibres

Trial of Strength

Most tissue functions are nonexistent in dead organisms. If individual muscle fibres are stored in cold dry conditions, they can maintain their strength and movement after many years. Stefan Galler of the Salzburg University Institute of Zoology undertook an experiment using the Iceman's muscle fibres to find out if they had retained this strength and movement. By comparing a tissue sample from his own leg with one from Ötzi's thigh, Galler discovered that the mummy's muscle fibres could still be stretched but did not contract. Effectively they were still intact – an astonishing result.

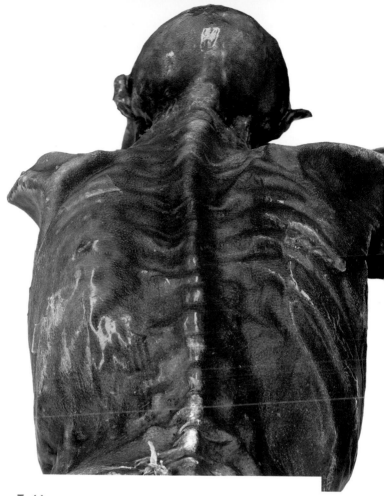

Tattoos

The Iceman's body displays over 50 tattoos in the form of groups of lines or crosses. Four groups of lines are located to the left of the spinal column, one to the right and three on the left calf. A further three are seen on the right instep and on the inner and outer ankle joint. A mark in the shape of a cross is located both on the back of the right knee and beside the left Achilles tendon. In contrast to modern tattoos, those of the Iceman were not carried out using needles but by means of fine incisions into which charcoal was rubbed. In India and Africa powdered charcoal is still used as a colouring to produce the characteristic bluish hue of tattoos.

Three of the four groups of lines located to the left of the spinal column

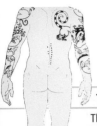

The tattoos of the nomad prince of Pazyryk. In addition to his decorative tattoos, he also displays signs of medical treatment that correspond exactly to those of Ötzi.

Timeless Tattoos

The existence of tattoos in ancient and early history is well known. A famous example is the Scythian nomad prince of Pazyryk from the Siberian Altai Mountains who lived around 400 BC. His magnificently tattooed body was preserved in the permafrost and, besides designs of a purely decorative nature, he also displays tattoos that were undertaken for therapeutic reasons, probably through branding. This technique is still used today.

Ötzi's tattoos are located at the precise points where his body was subjected to considerable strain during his lifetime and most likely caused him a lot of pain. The Iceman probably undertook this painful treatment on numerous occasions. Ötzi's tattoos are therefore not symbols but have a primarily painkilling function.

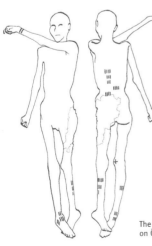

Astoundingly, the tattooed areas of the glacier mummy's body correspond to the pressure points known to acupuncturists today. In all probability this is the earliest example of acupuncture treatment known to man. Before Ötzi it was thought that this treatment had originated some two thousand years later in Asia.

The tattoos discovered on Ötzi's body

Stone Age Surgery

Late Stone Age people were obviously aware of a large number of natural substances that could be employed for therapeutic ends. Archaeologists have also confirmed the existence of surgical interventions at this time. For operations on the skull – so-called trepanation – four deep holes were drilled into the skull. Then, the bone in the resulting square was scraped off. It is, however, doubtful whether this brought any pain relief. There are finds which prove that patients treated in this manner survived the operation. Their skulls show that the aperture had closed again during the healing process.

A technical archaeologist knows no pain: Tattoos made with powdered charcoal like in Otzi's time

☞ Dorfer, L. et al.: 5200-Year-Old Acupuncture in Central Europe?
   In: Science (282) 5387/1998, pp. 242–243.
☞ Dorfer, L. et al.: A Medical Report from the Stone Age.
   In: The Lancet (354) 9183/1999, pp. 1023–1025.

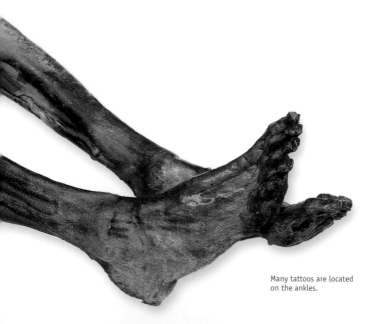

Many tattoos are located on the ankles.

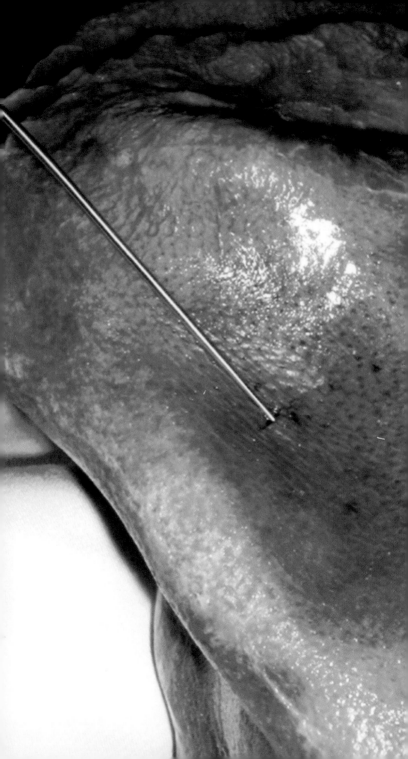

ÖTZI'S DEATH – A CRIMINAL CASE?

Shortly after Ötzi's discovery, rumours spread that the Iceman had been murdered. The tattoos on his wrist were taken for signs that he had been tied up and the 'hole' in his head as evidence of a violently inflicted head wound. The fact is that the back of the mummy's head was the first part of his body to be exposed to the sun, thus producing the destruction of a part of his scalp. Konrad Spindler took the unfinished and partly damaged nature of Ötzi's equipment as a sign that he had been the victim of an accident shortly before his death. He was also of the opinion that Ötzi had been on the run.

In July 2001, this theory could be partially confirmed: Ötzi died as a result of an arrow wound. On examining a series of new X-rays, Paul Gostner, radiologist at the Bolzano Hospital, discovered an arrowhead in the mummy's left shoulder. Computer tomography images show that the arrowhead created a two-cm hole in the left shoulder blade, ending up 15 mm from his lung. A more careful examination of the left-hand side of the mummy's back by pathologist Eduard Egarter Vigl, revealed a small skin wound. From this point, an unhealed canal made by the arrow leads into the interior of the body. Essential organs were not hit but in the arrow's trajectory lay the left arm's neuro-vascular fascicles which must have led to heavy bleeding and the possible laming of his arm.

Although there were initial doubts that the arrow wound had been deadly, it is clear today that it was – and that Ötzi died within a few minutes.

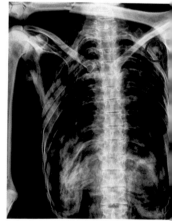

An X-ray of the thorax shows numerous bone fractures and – at the top right – the arrowhead.

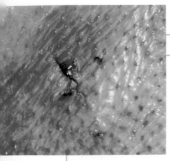

The stitched wound on the left shoulder

An Arrow in the Back

Paul Gostner, radiologist at the Bolzano Hospital, remarked, 'The discovery of the arrowhead revealed the cause of the Iceman's death. But this is not all. The mummy and the objects found with it have provided valuable information about these people and their culture. This latest discovery is clearly a further piece in this exciting puzzle and should be thought of as an incentive for further intensive archaeological research.'

The Iceman must have instinctively tried to remove the arrow from his back as it probably caused him great pain each time he moved. In this way the shaft was detached from the arrowhead.

The shape of the flint head that stuck in the Iceman's body corresponds to the typical stemmed surface-retouched Copper Age arrowheads of the Southern Alpine area. The Iceman too had such flint arrowheads in his quiver.

Traces of Blood

Examinations carried out by the Australian microbiologist Tom Loy show that traces of blood were present on one of Ötzi's arrow shafts, up to 30 cm from the tip. Blood was also found on the longbow, the dagger and the axe blade.

A new research programme initiated by the South Tyrol Archaeology Museum intends to take a closer look at Ötzi's equipment. Is there a chance that Ötzi placed his attacker's arrow shaft in his own quiver?

☞ Loy, T.: Blood on the Axe. Ötzi, the Man in the Ice. In: New Scientist 2151/1998, pp. 40–43.

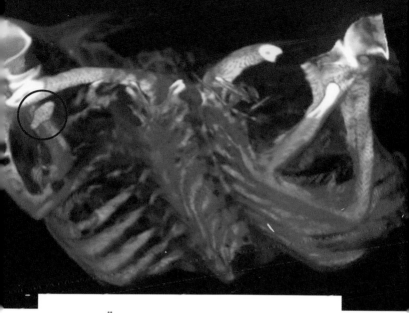

Computer tomography of the thorax: the arrowhead is clearly to be seen.

Why was Ötzi shot?

The exact circumstances of Ötzi's death will never be known. It is clear however that the Iceman was shot from behind, with his attacker standing lower down from him. Since the arrow did not go straight through him, it is highly likely that it was fired from a considerable distance. A deep cut on his right hand confirms that Ötzi was involved in hand-to-hand fighting immediately before his death.

Other questions remained unanswered however. Was he fleeing from someone or was the arrow in his back completely unexpected? Was anything stolen from him? At first sight nothing seems to be missing from Ötzi's equipment. Even his valuable axe with its copper blade – an attractive item for his attacker – was still there. Or was there something even more valuable? In many agrarian cultures and among nomadic peoples, herds represented a community's most cherished assets. If we assume that the Iceman was leading a herd of sheep or goats through this icy highland – and this would make him, ethnologically speaking, one of the leading members of his community – the theory of a theft of a herd cannot be entirely dismissed.

The copper blade axe is in all certainty a tool that belonged to elite members of society and indicates that the Iceman may also have been a warrior.

Death and Manslaughter 5,000 Years Ago

Warlike confrontations were frequent in the Copper Age and numerous weapon finds testify to this. Pictorial representations also show that communal life was not always very peaceful. Particularly eloquent is a Late Neolithic mass grave discovered in Talheim, near Heilbronn (Baden-Württenberg), Germany. The skulls of 34 men, women and children show signs of serious wounds caused by axe blows.

Sketch of the distribution of corpses in the Talheim mass grave

☞ Gleirscher, P.: Ausstattungselemente des Mannes aus dem Eis mit Blick auf Rangzeichen im kupferzeitlichen Mitteleuropa. In: Fleckinger, Angelika (Ed.): Die Gletschermumie aus der Kupferzeit 2. Neue Forschungsergebnisse zum Mann aus dem Eis/La mummia dell'età del rame 2. Nuove ricerche sull'Uomo venuto dal ghiaccio (Schriften des Südtiroler Archäologiemuseums 3). Wien/Bozen, Folio 2003, S. 41–57.

☞ Nisi, D./Nothdurfter, H.: Aufenthaltsspuren von Hirten über lange Zeiträume im Umkreis des Similaun. In: Fleckinger, Angelika (Ed.): Die Gletschermumie aus der Kupferzeit 2. Neue Forschungsergebnisse zum Mann aus dem Eis/La mummia dell'età del rame 2. Nuove ricerche sull'Uomo venuto dal ghiaccio (Schriften des Südtiroler Archäologiemuseums 3). Wien/Bozen, Folio 2003, S. 65–186.

☞ Wahl, J./König, H. G.: Anthropologisch-traumatologische Untersuchungen der menschlichen Skelettreste aus dem bandkeramischen Massengrab bei Talheim, Kreis Heilbronn. Fundbericht Baden-Württemberg 12/1987, pp. 65–186.

Johan Reinhard, an American archaeologist, believes that the case of the Iceman may represent a ritual execution or an offering to the gods. Ritual human sacrifices in high mountain areas are well known among the early cultures of Southern Peru, Chile and Argentina.

☞ Reinhard, J.: Who killed the Iceman? New find raises questions about prehistoric mummy. In: National Geographic 02/2002.

In the Alps, however, evidence of such ritual executions has not been discovered. The routine nature of the Iceman's 'burial' and the distance from which the deadly arrow was fired contradict such a theory.

Some details do however indicate a 'depositing' in the sense of a funeral. For instance the fact that the Iceman's possessions were 'laid out' in different spots around the rocky gully where he was found. A dead man could hardly have arranged his things in this way.

Furthermore much of his equipment is not usable. It may be that the dead man was provided with symbolically benign weaponry, such as bent swords or lances, for his journey into the next life. Such offerings are typical in ancient history. Were more people involved in this burial ceremony? Is that why the arrows in his quiver are so different?

This is one hypothesis among many but conclusive evidence is still lacking.

When did the Iceman die?

The time of Ötzi's death can be fairly accurately calculated, thanks to some of the smallest finds which lock together like pieces in a puzzle. The blossom of the hop bush is over by June and Ötzi's stomach contained pollen from this plant. The sloe berry found at the scene could have been harvested at any time between July and November. According to the chlorophyll levels found in the maple leaves in his birch-bark containers, these must have been freshly picked, sometime between June and September.

From this wealth of information, scientists have come to the conclusion that Ötzi must have died in the spring or early summer. By working together with scientists from widely diverse disciplines, the archaeologists were able to investigate aspects of the mummy's life that would otherwise have remained inaccessible.

Mummification

The exact steps in the mummification process have yet to be completely explained. Until the present, scientists have been unable to agree on one single theory. Among those put forward is the idea that Ötzi and his equipment were covered with a protective layer of snow, which over the years permitted air to filter through yet kept the corpse dry. After many years, the ice of the glacier covered the mummy and so the mummification process – a form of freeze-drying – came to an end.

Another theory holds that mummification took place without the protective layer of snow but simply on the bare ground or in the melt water, the corpse being later covered in snow and ice. This, however, seems unlikely, as the corpse would have been exposed to insects and especially predators. Furthermore the absence of snow cover would have altered the position of the carefully laid out items of equipment. The birch-bark containers in particular would have been blown away by the wind.

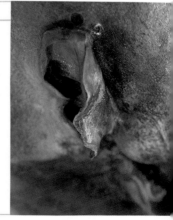

Ötzi's left ear is folded over

The Position

The position in which the Iceman was found was probably the one in which he died. Especially noteworthy is the unnatural pose of his left arm. The shoulder joint is dislocated. Furthermore the left ear is folded forward and the nose and upper lip are stretched up to the right. These observations confirm that the movement of the glacier ice must have caused slight changes in the mummy's position.

skimo baby

MUMMIES FROM ALL OVER THE WORLD

There are numerous naturally and artificially mummified corpses in existence. Most of them were found in graves.

The Iceman is the oldest mummy in the world. Both his extraordinary age and the type of mummification make him particularly valuable for scientists. Ötzi is a so-called 'damp mummy' i.e. one in which humidity is retained in individual cells. The body tissue is therefore elastic and suitable for performing many different scientific experiments.

Tollund Man

Most of the mummies known to us come from Egypt. These are corpses whose brains and internal organs were removed during the burial ritual and the skin treated with substances to guarantee their conservation. In contrast, the Iceman appears to have been snatched from the living, unchanged by burial rituals or other interventions.

Another case of natural mummification is the corpse of a 500-year-old Inuit baby found in 1972 along with other mummies beneath a rocky outcrop in Greenland. This corpse was freeze-dried by the icy Arctic winds.

There are also many cases of mummies conserved in turf bogs, most of which date from after Christ. The most well known is undoubtedly the splendidly conserved Tollund Man from Denmark.

The Chancay culture (Central Peru) wrapped their dead in textiles or palm matting in a sitting position and dried them in the sun.

A fine example of a bound and tied mummy is the so-called Prince of El Plomo, discovered by shepherds on the peak of the Chilean mountain El Plomo in 1954. This is an approximately 500-year-old Inca relic of an eight or nine-year-old body sacrificed to the gods. The mummy and other fascinating finds are today exhibited at the Museum of Natural History in Santiago, Chile.

The Prince of El Plomo

The Prince of El Plomo

According to Sonia Guillén of the Bioanthropology Foundation, Peru, 'The mummy is in an outstanding state of conservation. Extensive scientific research in 1982 produced revealing information on the child's state of health and the cause of death.

The boy was elaborately laid out for the sacrifice, dressed in fine clothes and had jewellery on his head that included numerous headbands. Among the sacrificial gifts offered to the gods were classic Inca artefacts such as human figures, ceramics, textiles and wooden objects.'

THE CLOTHING

At the time of his death, Ötzi was fully clothed and lay on his stomach on a large flat stone. First to be exposed to the air was his back so that the clothing in this area was blown away by the strong winds prevalent at this altitude. The garments that covered his chest and stomach were, however, preserved.

The Iceman finds offer us a previously unavailable glimpse into the daily life of a Copper Age inhabitant of the Alps. Under normal conservation conditions, items of clothing and equipment made of organic materials would not have survived.

How far Ötzi's clothing can be considered typical is difficult to assess due to the lack of comparable items. Thanks to the painstaking work of restorers, individual garments could be reconstructed from a large number of small pieces.

The clothing consists of a cap, upper garments, leggings, a belt, a loincloth, a pair of shoes and a grass cape.

None of the clothing was made of woven materials but of tanned hides and grass strands. Animal sinews were used for sewing and to a lesser extent dried grass and tree bast.

Materials for his Clothing		
Type of Animal	**Material**	**Garment**
Domestic goat	Hide	Upper garments, leggings, loincloth
Brown bear	Hide	Cap, shoe soles
Deer	Hide	Shoe uppers, legging straps
Calf	Leather	Belt and pouch

The Iceman with reconstructed
clothing and equipment

Archaeological Rarities

Remains of clothing are rare archaeological finds. Up to now only examples made of plant fibres had been found. In contrast to hide garments, these remained intact on the damp ground of the pile dwellings of the Alpine region. Ötzi's belt, sandals and cap provide a vivid picture of Late Stone Age weaving and knotting techniques.

The Restoration of the Finds

Shortly after the discovery of the glacier mummy, signs of drying out were noticed in the organic materials. Contact was immediately established with the Römisch-Germanisches Zentralmuseum in Mainz, Germany so that it should assume responsibility for the appropriate storage and conservation measures that these finds required.

The work undertaken by the Mainz museum lasted three years. After being thoroughly catalogued, samples were taken from each of the finds in order to ascertain the nature of their materials.

Finds made of leather, grass, tree bast and wood were first cleaned with distilled water and then submerged in a special solution to reduce the expansion caused by water on freezing. By finally freeze-drying the objects, the ice could be removed without altering the cell structure.

The numerous small pieces were assembled and slowly a picture of the clothing and equipment emerged.

The choice of materials and their preparation is proof that Stone Age people were extraordinarily skilled at adapting to their environment.

The grass matting soon after the discovery

Grass Cape, Mat or Backpack?

During the second examination of the scene of the find, three large sections of matting made of Alpine swamp grass were uncovered. These woven objects were at first taken to be a sleeveless cape worn over his hide clothing. Doubts have since emerged about this theory. If the Iceman had really used this weave as a cape, the shoulder area would have been much wider – which was not the case. The original theory about how it was actually worn gives rise to further practical problems. The backpack and quiver would either have been carried under or over this 'coat' but the quiver would have quickly worn the grass matting away.

Most likely the Iceman wore the matting over his head, fastening it with the aid of string at the top. Ethnological comparisons show that shepherd peoples used similar mats as effective protection from the rain.

It is also possible that the matting was a part of the backpack but straps to fasten it to the frame are missing.

Barth, R.: Neuer Deutungsversuch zu dem beim Mann aus dem Eis vorgefundenen mattenartigen Grasfragment. In: Fleckinger, Angelika (Ed.): Die Gletschermumie aus der Kupferzeit 2. Neue Forschungsergebnisse zum Mann aus dem Eis/La mummia dell'età del rame 2. Nuove ricerche sull'Uomo venuto dal ghiaccio (Schriften des Südtiroler Archäologiemuseums 3). Wien/Bozen, Folio 2003, S. 23–27.

The Hide Coat

Ötzi's coat was made of the hide of the domestic goat. The individual sections were carefully cross-stitched together. Darker strips alternate with lighter ones and the stitching was done with the fibres of animal sinews.

The Iceman wore the coat with the fur on the outside. The fur itself most probably largely fell out when the garment dried out.

On the inner side, numerous signs of scraping are visible, probably from the process of cleaning the skin. Scientific examinations indicate the presence of remains of fat and smoke.

His garments had been used over a long period of time as can be seen from the dirt on the inner side, sweat marks and several repairs using grass fibres. A reconstruction of the coat shows that the Iceman wore the coat with the front open. A fastening is however missing, but in all likelihood, he used his belt to keep it closed. While a few horizontal hide strips have survived from the shoulder area, nothing remains of the sleeves. It is therefore unclear whether the coat actually had sleeves.

Stone Age Fashion

Hide clothes with long strips remind us of the menhirs and stele of the Southern Alpine area. Female stele have breasts and are adorned with jewellery. The male versions feature necklaces, diverse weapons and also items of clothing, including striped hide coats and belts.

By stele we mean monoliths in human forms erected to celebrate high-ranking members of the community. This can be seen from both the weaponry and the clothing, which possibly had a ritual meaning.

The Leggings

The two separate leggings are made of several pieces of domestic goat hide cross-stitched together. 65 cm long, these leggings covered only the thigh and calf. The bow-shaped top was rein-forced with a leather strip that was threaded through it. Two laces were sewn on to each legging so that they could be knotted onto the belt. At the lower end, deerskin laces were sewn on which were then tied to the shoes to prevent the leggings from riding up as the Iceman walked. The leggings show signs of heavy use and fre-quent repairs.

It should be mentioned that Ötzi's leggings are the oldest garment of their kind in the world.

Leggings

The shape of the two separate leggings was absolutely practical and functional. Native North Americans were still using such leggings in the 19th century.

The Belt and Pouch

The belt was made of a 4–4.8-cm strip of calf's leather and the pouch of a piece of sewn-on leather. The longest open side was strengthened by decorative stitching and could be closed with a fine leather thong. The remaining fragments show that the belt was originally almost two metres long and could be wound twice around the hips.

This little pouch contained a scraper, a drill and a flint flake. A 7.1-cm bone awl was also found.

A Universal Tool

The technical archaeologist Harm Paulsen described the awl as a 'multifunctional tool. It could be used for anything from sewing to making tattoos or simply as a tooth pick. Ötzi's clothes were definitely not sewn using a needle with an eye. The needle and the double width of the sinew fibres would have left an excessively large hole. Holes could be made using the awl and the sinews later threaded through.'

Ötzi's awl, made from the bone of an animal's foot

The Iceman used his belt-pouch to keep his valuable tools safe. The only other item found inside was a black lump, later identified as true tinder fungus.

Ötzi's Lighter

The flesh of the true tinder fungus (Fomes fomentarius) is ideal for lighting fires and must therefore be kept absolutely dry.

True tinder fungus

The fungus shows slight traces of iron pyrites and proves that Ötzi knew how to use this mineral to produce sparks. Iron pyrites, or fool's gold, is an extremely hard mineral that produces sparks when it strikes flint. When the sparks land on a bed of fluffy tinder fungus that has been previously enriched with some kind of nitrogen such as urine, it begins to glow. By adding easily inflammable material and blowing, it starts to burn. It only takes a minute to start a fire in this way.

The Loin Cloth

This 50-cm-long, 33-cm-wide garment was made of long narrow strips of goat's leather cross-stitched together.
Originally measuring around one metre, this cloth was worn between the legs and fastened to the belt. The longer frontal part hung over the belt and protected the contents of the belt pouch from the damp.

The Shoes

The Iceman's shoes are the oldest 'real' shoes ever found. When the mummy was taken to the Innsbruck Anatomical Institute, his right shoe was still on his foot, but had to be removed for restoration.
The structure of the shoes is extremely functional and refined and consists of an inner and outer part.

Ötzi's foot shortly after the recovery with the right shoe still in place

The inner shoe is composed of tree bast netting holding in place the hay that served as insulation material. The outer part is made of deerskin. Both sections – the tree bast netting and the leather upper – are fastened to an oval-shaped sole made of bearskin by means of leather straps. In contrast to the sole, the uppers were worn with the fur on the outside. The upper part was closed using a form of shoelaces. The shaft around the ankle was bound with tree bast fibres to prevent the damp from getting in. A strip of leather was attached diagonally across the sole in order to give it some kind of grip.

Ötzi's shoes:
the complete
right shoe
and the
netting of the
left shoe

On the road in Ötzi's shoes

Experiments undertaken by the technical archaeologist Anne Reichert who reconstructed Iceman's shoes show that the leather strip running diagonally across the sole really did prevent slipping on rocky ground. The shoes are surprisingly warm and comfortable, however they are not suitable for walking in the rain as water comes in through the slits in the soles.

 Reichert, A.: Zur Rekonstruktion der „Ötzi"-Schuhe. In: Experimentelle Archäologie. Bilanz 1999, Oldenburg 2000, pp. 69–76.

Reconstruction of
the sole

Reconstruction of
the leather upper

Reconstruction of
the shoe netting

The Bearskin Cap

During the second archaeological excavation, Ötzi's headgear was found where his head had lain.

It consists of a semi-spherical bearskin cap made up of several pieces of hide. In this case, the outer fur was perfectly conserved. On the lower edge, two leather straps were attached that must have been tied under the chin to keep the cap in place. Both chinstraps were already torn before Ötzi's death.

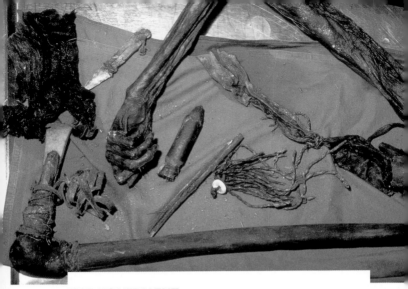

THE EQUIPMENT

The Iceman possessed an extremely varied and useful selection of equipment, which enabled him to spend long periods away from home, and take care of his varying needs.

Using his tools, he was able to repair damaged items and produce entirely new ones.

In all probability, Ötzi only carried his bow in his hand and transported the rest of his equipment in his backpack, belt and quiver. This was the only way he could negotiate difficult terrain.

Materials for his Equipment		
Type of animal	**Material**	**Use**
Chamois	Hide	Quiver
Deer	Antler	Spike for retoucheur, big spike, our points
Cow or deer	Sinews	Sinews for thread or strings
Bird	Feathers	Feather for arrows
Goat, sheep, chamois or ibex	Bones	Awls

The Axe

The most important item of the Iceman's equipment is his copper blade axe. It is the only completely intact prehistoric axe in the world.

The blade is trapeziform in shape, measuring 9.5 cm and made of 99.7% pure copper with traces of arsenic and silver. The narrow ends have slightly raised edges and the carefully smoothed yew haft is around 60 cm long. At the top of the haft there is a forked shaft into which the blade was fixed with birch tar and then tightly bound with thin leather straps to keep it stable.

Signs of Sharpening

According to Dr. Gilberto Artioli of the Geosciences Department of the University of Milan, 'Working groups from the universities of Milan and Trento examined the Iceman's axe and others from the same period. Using thermal neutrons and high-energy X-rays – obtained from particle accelerators, so-called synchrotrons – the copper crystal structure within the axe blade can be made visible without damaging the blade itself. In this way, the manufacture of the axe can be accurately reconstructed.

Variations in structure indicate that the blade's density was altered by sharpening.'

Weapon, Tool or Status Symbol?

Technical archaeologist Harm Paulsen uses a replica of Ötzi's axe to fell a yew tree in 45 minutes.

According to the technical archaeologist Harm Paulsen, 'Due to the softness of the metal, the axe was originally thought to be useless as a tool or a weapon. However experimental archaeology has shown that the axe was ideal for felling trees. Without having to sharpen the blade once, I was able to fell a yew tree in around 45 minutes. Obviously the axe has to be used differently from modern steel axes. Instead of one powerful blow, three separate fine chops have to be made with Ötzi's axe.'

The axe blade

The axe was certainly not exclusively a status symbol or a symbolic object – the cutting edge shows clear signs of use.
In the period around 3000 years BC, copper axes belonged to men of the highest echelons of society and were also used as weapons. Could the Iceman have been a tribal leader or a warrior?

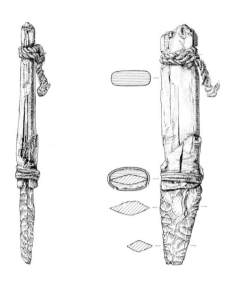

The Dagger and Sheath

The 13-cm-long dagger is made up of a small triangular flint blade and an ash wood handle. Researchers have ascertained that the flint comes from the quarries of the Lessini Mountains, east of Lake Garda, Italy. If the blade had been found without the handle, it would have probably been taken for an arrowhead. The blade was forced deep into the wooden handle and bound with animal sinews. A string was attached to a notch at the end of the handle.

The triangular sheath-like scabbard belonging to the dagger is 12 cm long. It is made of a mesh of tree bast and sewn along the longest side with grass fibres. Double plaiting reinforces the opening of the sheath and horizontal wefts in twisted yarn are worked into the sheath at regular intervals. It is a remarkably fine object, elaborated with considerable care. On one side, a leather eye presumably allowed the sheath to be attached to the belt, making it accessible whenever it was needed.

Flint

Sectional view of
the retoucheur

The Retoucheur

This approximately 12-cm-long tool is made of a piece of lime
wood branch with the bark removed, cut straight at one end and
shaped to a point at the other. At the pointed end an approximately 6-cm-long rod was hammered into the medullar canal,
leaving about 4 mm protruding. On closer examination, the rod
turned out to be a fire-hardened stag's antler.

As no such object had previously been found, this pencil-like tool
proved to be something of a mystery. Finally archaeologists discovered that it could be used for detailed work in the manufacture
of flint instruments.

At first a lump of flint would be hammered into a desired shape,
just as in the manufacture of raw blades. The next step was to use
this special tool to carry out precision work by means of pressing.

The retoucheur is particularly appropriate for
sharpening flint blades.

When the retoucheur's point became blunt, it
could be sharpened much like a modern pencil
and reused.

Using the hardened point, fine mussel-like
splinters could be pressed out of a raw blade.

The Longbow

The largest item the Iceman possessed was a 1.82-cm longbow made of yew. Signs of carving show that it was not entirely finished. The original piece of wood, cut from a tree trunk using his axe, clearly shows the type of bow Ötzi was attempting to fashion. The finished bow would have been rubbed down and polished using field horsetail – a poisonous herb – to achieve a smooth surface. In prehistoric bows, the bowstring is usually attached to one end of the bow by means of a loop and bound at the other. There is no sign, however, of Ötzi's bowstring.

When the Australian molecular biologist Tom Loy removed the bow stave from the cold chamber at the Römisch-Germanisches National Museum, he immediately noticed an unpleasantly rancid smell. Loy's examination confirmed that the bow stave was drenched in blood. This can be explained in two ways: either the dried blood was deliberately smeared on the bow as it is a known water-repellent, or the blood came from the injury Ötzi sustained on his hand.

The ball of string found in the quiver could not have been Ötzi's bowstring, as was originally thought.

Detail of the bow stave

Technical archaeologist Harm
Paulsen testing a reconstruction
of Ötzi's longbow.

Master Bowman

According to Paulsen, 'I created a new bow using Ötzi's as a model and tried it out. My experiment showed that the bow could only achieve the required elasticity if it is made in part of sap wood. Trials have demonstrated that wild animals can easily be shot from a distance of 30–50 m with considerable accuracy. A stag or a roe deer can be shot straight through at a distance of 30 m. The bow can in fact reach distances of up to 180 m. Ötzi's longbow therefore possesses the same characteristics as a modern sport bow. Pulled to a distance of 72 cm, the weight on the fingers is equivalent to approximately 28 kg.'

The Quiver and its Contents

The quiver is made of a rectangular, elongated hide bag that tapers slightly towards the bottom.

The piece of hide was held together lengthways and supported by a 92.2-cm-long hazel wood rod. This supporting strut had already been broken into three sections during Ötzi's lifetime. The lid and the carrying strap were missing. The elaborately decorated side pocket remains in good condition however.

The quiver contained twelve rough arrow shafts and two finished arrows. The unfinished shafts are between 84 and 87 cm long and made of the shoots of viburnum sapwood. Their bark had been removed but not yet smoothed down and all had notches cut into the ends.

Both finished arrows have flint arrowheads, fixed to the shaft with birch tar and then bound with thread. These arrows are unique in that the shafts display the remains of three-part radial fletching, attached with birch tar and bound with thin nettle fibres. This fletching served to stabilize the arrow during flight. One of the arrows had an extended shaft made of cornel wood inserted into the top.

The quiver also held four tips of stag antlers tied together with strips of bast. There was also a bent antler tip that the iceman probably used for skinning the animals he had hunted. Besides two animal sinews, there was also a ball of tree bast string some two metres long. The irregular and inelastic nature of this cord makes it unlikely that it could have served as a bowstring.

One of the two finished arrows found in Ötzi's quiver

A Left-Hander?

'The Iceman's finished arrows,' according to technical archaeologist Harm Paulsen, 'could not have been made by the same
person. The fletching shows that
one was wound by a left-hander
and the other by a right-hander.
Furthermore, the arrow with the
extended tip was too long for the
Iceman's quiver.'

The feather sections
were glued with
birch tar then
spirally bound.

Stag antler

Animal sinews

Stag antler tips

Reconstruction of
the backpack

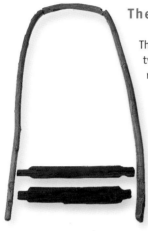

The Backpack

The frame of the backpack consists of a two-metre-long U-shaped hazel wood rod and two narrow wooden boards measuring 38 and 40.3 cm. The latter probably served as a horizontal connection between the two sides of the frame, originally tied together with string. Numerous remnants of this string were found beside the two boards. A few pieces of hide and clumps of hair tend to indicate that a hide sack was attached to the frame to carry the Iceman's possessions.

The Net

This roughly meshed net made of tree bast string was probably used for catching birds and rabbits.
Rabbits would be driven into the net before being clubbed to death.

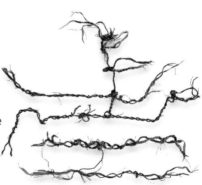

Rabbit Hunting

Nets used for hunting are shown in illustrated bronze receptacles from the Late Iron Age (5th century BC) such as the one found in Certosa, near Bologna, Italy and another from Welzelach (East Tyrol).

The Birch-Bark Containers

The two birch-bark containers found at the scene are shaped in the form of cylindrical pots. The slightly oval-shaped base has a diameter of 15–18 cm. The body of the container measures around 20 cm and is made of a single right-angled piece of birch-bark. The base was sewn to the body with tree bast.

The interior of one of the containers was blackened, leading experts to believe it had been used for transporting the embers of fires. This container also held freshly picked maple leaves peppered with traces of charcoal. The leaves were used as insulation material in order to keep the embers burning for short periods of time so that a new fire could be made quickly.

Birch-bark containers were much lighter than ceramic vessels and far less fragile.

Ötzi's flint drill

A flint instrument for cutting, scraping, planing and polishing

Razor sharp blades for cutting and carving

Minerals and Tools

Ötzi was in possession of 18 different types of wood, which enabled him to produce a variety of tools. Bark was used for making containers and tree bast for string and thread. Dried grasses were also used for making items of clothing. The Iceman was evidently capable of making new objects and restoring damaged ones without any exterior help.

Indeed he was skilled at both recognizing the raw materials available to him and at using them to their best advantage in order to survive in his environment. Such skills have been largely lost today.

The Stone Disc

This disc made of Dolomite marble has a hole in the
middle through which a hide strip is threaded. Through a
loop in this strip, nine further twisted hide strips are tied
on, forming a sort of tassel.

The disc's function remains a mystery but the hide strips may well
have been a valuable source of repair material. However, in damp
conditions or with clammy hands, it would have been extremely
difficult to untie the strips. The stone disc would make the task
of untying them easier.

 Greiff, S./Banerjee, A.: Mineralogische Untersuchungen am Amulett
der Ötztaler Gletscherleiche mithilfe der Diffusen IR-Reflexionsspektro-
skopie. In: Arch. Korrespondenzblatt 23/1993, pp. 461–466.

The Stone Disc on the Belt?

Technical archaeologist Anne Reichert says that, 'Experiments prove that the hide tassel can be attached to the belt by threading the stone disc under the belt. In pocket-less garments such as the Japanese kimono, bags were often attached to the belt with the aid of a stone disc.'

Ötzi's First-Aid Kit

Among his possessions, the Iceman also carried a modest first-aid kit.

Two pieces of the flesh of the birch fungus polyphore had been cut and threaded on to separate hide strings. In all probability they were used for therapeutic ends. Up until modern times, tree fungus has been used for curing a variety of medical conditions. It is known that birch fungus has antibiotic and styptic effects. Furthermore, the toxic oils in tree fungi are effective against the intestinal parasites that Ötzi himself suffered from.

☞ Capasso, L.: 5300 years ago, the Ice Man used natural laxatives and antibiotics. In: The Lancet 352 9143/1998, p. 1864.

life-size statue with carved
weapons and clothing found at
Algund, South Tyrol

A DEAD MAN SPEAKS OF LIFE

A Time of Upheaval

The Late Neolithic period is also known as the Copper Age in order to differentiate it from the merely agriculturally oriented Early Neolithic period.

This was a time of great upheavals, in which mineral extraction and copper smelting required enormous advances in both mining and technical know how.

Mineral extraction began in Anatolia and the Caucasus where, as early as 6,000 years BC, copper had already been smelted. By 4000 BC, Near Eastern techniques of copper smelting had already reached Central Europe by way of the Balkans and the Mediterranean.

Late Neolithic discoveries of new metals such as copper, gold and silver and the development of metal work-

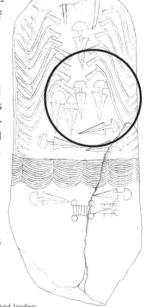

ing techniques brought about considerable changes within the structure of society. Different social groups were created and society took on a hierarchical nature for the first time. Moreover, the search for new mineral deposits and the exchange of finished goods encouraged cultural exchanges over large areas. Objects made of copper took on a symbolic meaning and laid down criteria of status, power and wealth.

In all, it can be assumed that at this time the region of the Alps was heavily settled by numerous cultural groups from the surrounding areas, attracted by the economic possibilities offered by its rich copper deposits.

Menhir of a man showing status symbols of warriors and leaders such as axes and daggers similar to those of Ötzi.

Which cultural group did Ötzi belong to?

Grave at Remedello

In itself, the uniqueness of the find makes its cultural classification extremely problematic. The lack of ceramics in particular makes the task even more difficult. Only Ötzi's weaponry can truly be compared and evaluated in sociological terms.

Based on the meagre Copper Age finds discovered in what is today the South Tyrol, everything indicates that he should be classified as a member of the first independent Alpine cultural group, 'Tamins-Carasso-Isera 5'. Emerging during the last centuries of the fourth millennium BC, this group is characterized by simple ceramic vessels with edging, notches and rows of dots. Their burial ritual consisted of mass graves in caves or rocky ledges.

Also influential was the Remedello Culture, which existed in the Po Valley at the same time. It takes its name from the graveyard of Remedello Sotto, south west of Lake Garda. The graves consist of simple oval-shaped earth mounds. Buried along with the men were arrowheads, daggers, axes and items of jewellery. Clear social differentiation can be seen: only 17% of the axes and 13% of the daggers possessed copper blades.

Menhirs of women (this one was found at Algund, South Tyrol) show breasts and items of jewellery, never weapons.

The remaining axe blades and daggers are made of either ophite or flint. Notably the finds in grave 102 at Remedello, somewhat older than the Iceman find, are comparable with Ötzi's equipment. Among the male bodies buried in this grave, a copper blade axe, a dagger and several flint arrowheads were found.

Among the other cultural groups existing in Ötzi's time were the Horgen culture in Switzerland and the Baden culture in Austria. In Bavaria, the Chamer culture extended as far the Inn Valley of the Tyrol.

☞ De Marinis, R.: The eneolithic cementery of Remedello Sotto (BS) and the relative and absolute chronology of the Copper Age in Northern Italy. In: Notiziario Archeologico Bergomenese 5/1998, pp. 41–59.
☞ Pedrotti, A.: L'età del Rame. In: Storia del Trentino I. La preistoria e la protostoria. Bologna, Il Mulino 2000, pp. 183–253.

What language did the Iceman speak?

It is almost certain that Late Stone Age people were able to articulate aspects of their environment verbally and pass on complex information. Only by means of language could Neolithic man have joined forces and undertaken projects which for an individual would have been impossible.

Although the first form of writing developed around 3500 BC in Mesopotamia, the first evidence of writing in the Alps dates from around 500 BC, in the Late Iron Age.

Herding the Sheep

Farmers from the Italian Vinschgau still herd their sheep over the Alps to the high pastures of the Ötz Valley in Austria where they retain grazing rights.
Transhumance therefore dates back over 5,000 years.

ven today the farmers of the Italian
chnals Valley drive their sheep
p to the Ötz Valley in Austria.

Transhumance

Besides agriculture, cattle breeding was vital to the Neolithic economy. Domestic animals at that time included sheep, goats, pigs, cows and dogs.

Sheep and goats, the oldest farm animals kept by humans, are more useful and more likely to survive winters in high mountain environments than cattle. There is no evidence of haymaking in the Late Stone Age, so straw and foliage must have been collected to feed cattle over the winter period.

In summer sheep and goats are driven up to the mountain pastures. This form of agriculture is known as transhumance. Pollen profiles indicate that Alpine pastures above the forest line have been used as grazing land for between 6,000 and 6,500 years.

During the time of the Iceman, the Ötz Valley must have had extensive areas of grazing land, even though the forest limit, due to better climatic conditions, lay at around 2,200–2,300 m above sea level. The usable land above the forest line was clearly artificially extended along the valley, especially by means of forest clearance.

The finds that accompanied the Iceman make it clear that, despite the existence of domestic animals, people at that time also hunted mountain goats, red deer, chamois and bears. The fruits of hunting were not exclusively edible but used for the production of clothing and tools.

Bortenschlager, S.: Die Umwelt des Mannes aus dem Eis und sein Einfluss darauf. In: Die Gletschermumie aus der Kupferzeit. Neue Forschungsergebnisse zum Mann aus dem Eis. Schriften des Südtiroler Archäologiemuseums 1. Bozen 1999, pp. 81–95.

Where did the Iceman live?

The flintstone from the area of Lake Garda, the typology of his axe, the choice of wood for his equipment and the pollen in his intestines all indicate that the Iceman must have lived somewhere south of the Alpine mountain chain.

Pollen as an indicator

The Botanical Institute of the University of Innsbruck analysed the Iceman's stomach contents and identified 30 different types of pollen, the majority of which were types of tree pollen. The types of trees involved indicate that he came from an area of mixed woodland such as the Vinschgau or the Schnals Valley. Important evidence as to the Iceman's place of residence is supplied by the presence of pollen from the hop hornbeam. This tree only grows south of the Alps and is particularly extensive in the Vinschgau. Judging by the degree to which the pollen had been digested, botanists believe that Ötzi must have been down in the Vinschgau twelve hours before his death.

One of Ötzi's arrow shafts was made of cherry dogwood, a tree that grows principally south of the main Alpine mountain chain.

The isotopic composition of Ötzi's tooth enamel proves that the Iceman did not spend his early childhood in a limestone area. This is further evidence that his homeland was in the Vinschgau or the lower Eisack Valley.

Numerous recent archaeological excavations on the castle hill of Schloss Juval at the beginning of the Schnals Valley have unearthed Neolithic and Bronze Age remains in what appears to be a settlement. Could this have been home to the Iceman?

Moss provides clues as to Ötzi's place of residence

James H. Dickson of Glasgow University, 'Ethnological comparisons show that moss was used as insulation material, toilet paper and for healing wounds. Its acid content has an antiseptic effect.'

Numerous samples of moss and lichens were collected from the melt water in the rocky gully where the Iceman was found and also from his clothes. Of the 75 types accounted for, only half of these still grow in the high mountain. Types found such as Neckera, N. crispa and N. complana are typical of the Schnals Valley and the Vinschgau.

The Schnals Valley, looking towards the main Alpine range.

What did Ötzi have for lunch?

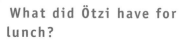

Einkorn, a precursor of modern day wheat

An examination of the Iceman's stomach contents revealed that his last meal consisted of einkorn porridge, meat and some unidentifiable vegetables. Among the remains of food were charcoal particles and minerals. We can therefore safely conclude that this meal was cooked on an open fire. The corn had been well chewed and was possibly eaten in the form of bread. In the hide scraps of his clothing two grains of corn were found – einkorn. These were probably not from a food he brought with him but must have accidentally found their way up to the Tisenjoch.

Parasites

The stomach examination also revealed the presence of the eggs of whipworm (Trichuris trichiura) and proves that the Iceman suffered from these parasites. Serious cases can lead to diahorrea and stomach pains. An estimated 20–70% of the world population are affected by whipworm today.

Ötzi's varied diet also included dried wild plums, wild apples, edible fungi and berries. At the scene of the find, a sloe berry was discovered. While it is not a particularly nutritious fruit, it is rich in vitamins and minerals and helps ward off thirst.

The anatomical and zoological analysis of two tiny bone splinters has shown that they come from part of the vertebra of a male mountain goat. The Iceman had probably taken along provisions for his journey consisting of smoked or dried mountain goat meat.

Who was the Iceman?

In the Copper Age, possession of objects made of copper or precious metals undoubtedly denoted membership of the warrior or leadership class. Proof that copper axes and daggers were status symbols is provided by the human-like stone statues of that time. The Iceman and his family probably had considerable status within their community and may well have been cattle owners, chiefs or village representatives.

To judge from his equipment, he may also have been a hunter. There again, hunting may only have been one of his many daily activities.

Another hypothesis suggests that Ötzi could well have been a trader of some sort, since his body was found on a north-south passage and it is known that Late Stone Age people bartered raw materials and goods. However, nothing among his possessions can be considered goods for trading.

Was Ötzi a mineral prospector? The Alpine region with its numerous copper deposits was definitely the destination of mineral prospectors. Ötzi, however, had neither the appropriate tools nor mineral samples with him.

The fact that much of his equipment was either broken or badly in need of repair supports the theory that the Iceman had been banished from his community and for this reason found himself in such inhospitable terrain. The idea that Ötzi was a shaman – since these people often lived outside established society – is contradicted by the lack of ritual objects.

THE SOUTH TYROL MUSEUM OF ARCHAEOLOGY IN BOLZANO

Opened on March 28, 1998, the South Tyrol Museum of Archaeology in Bolzano (South Tyrol) documents the ancient and early history of the South Tyrol from the end of the last Ice Age (15000 BC) up to the time of Charlemagne (800 AD) over an area of 1,200 m². The Iceman and his possessions are the centrepiece of the museum.

Furthermore, the whole story of the discovery, recovery, excavations and medical examinations is told by means of display boards, video projections and interactive media. The finds are kept in specially air-conditioned cabinets at a temperature of 18°C and illuminated with 50 lux. The mummy itself can be seen through a small tank glass window. Numerous illustrations and 1:1 scale drawings testify to the handicraft skills of Copper Age man.

For the journey to Bolzano, the mummy was transported in a refrigerated van.

The Journey Back

On January 16, 1998, the mummy and the rest of the finds were transported from the Anatomical Institute of the University of Innsbruck to the South Tyrol Museum of Archaeology in Bolzano amid unprecedented security measures and extraordinary media interest.

The border at the Brenner Pass

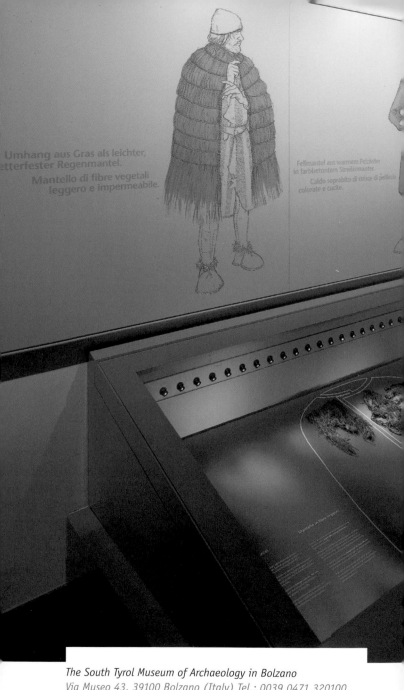

Umhang aus Gras als leichter, wetterfester Regenmantel.

Mantello di fibre vegetali leggero e impermeabile.

Fellmantel aus warmem Pelzleder in farbbetontem Streifenmuster.

Caldo soprabito di strisce di pelliccia colorate e cucite.

Mantello in fibre vegetali

The South Tyrol Museum of Archaeology in Bolzano
Via Museo 43, 39100 Bolzano (Italy) Tel.: 0039 0471 320100
museum@iceman.it, www.iceman.it

*Open daily (except Mondays) 10am–5pm,
Thursdays 10am–7pm, closed January 1, May 1 and December 25.*

Inside the
South Tyrol
Museum of
Archaeology

Conservation at the South Tyrol Museum of Archaeology

During the six years that the mummy spent in the Anatomical Institute of the University of Innsbruck, he was wrapped in a sterile operating gown and laid on a bed of crushed ice.

In order to put the Iceman on display at the South Tyrol Museum of Archaeology, an entirely new cooling system had to be developed.

The so-called 'Iceman Box' is a unique installation composed of two cold chambers, each with independent systems, an examination room and a decontamination cell at the entrance.

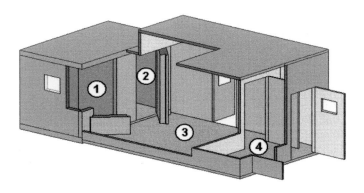

① The cold cell with a temperature of −6°C and air humidity of 98%
② Reserve cold cell with a temperature of −6°C and air humidity of 98%
③ Examination room with temperatures varying between −6°C and room temperature
④ Decontamination cell

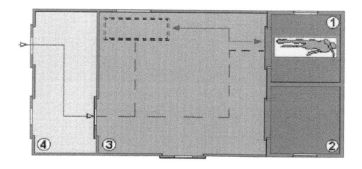

Ötzi under the Sprinkler

Eduard Egarter Vigl, the pathologist responsible for the mummy's conservation at the South Tyrol Museum of Archaeology, remarked that, 'The mummy's maintenance is a tightrope walk between conservation requirements and the need to make the mummy visible in the museum. In order to prevent it from losing its natural humidity, I developed a new system. By sprinkling the body with sterilized water, a thin film of ice builds up on the surface. The circulation of humidity within the cold cell therefore only affects the artificial layer of ice on the surface and not the body tissue.'

Through a window measuring 40 x 40 cm, visitors to the museum can take a look inside the cold cell where the mummy is laid out on precision scales and conserved at a temperature of −6°C and 98% air humidity.

Refrigeration system

All rooms are sterilized and the air is filtered. There is a small laboratory available for scientific examinations. A computer system records values such as air pressure, temperature, relative humidity and body weight by means of sonars attached to the mummy itself and inside the cold cell. Whenever variations are recorded, an alarm goes off automatically. This security system alerts in-house specialist staff and Dr Egarter Vigl who can take immediate action.

Under Control

According to Marco Samadelli, a technician at the South Tyrol Museum of Archaeology, 'By means of a system of optical and electronic instruments, it can be scientifically ensured that the mummy is being conserved in optimum conditions. Regular tests held approximately once a month photograph a section of the mummy's skin measuring around 1.5 cm^2. The images obtained can then be compared with existing photographs. Using special software, minute changes in the luminosity, colour and deformation of the skin can be distinguished. Since bacteria or decomposition processes cause skin deformations, the state of the mummy can be constantly assessed.

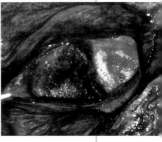

Ötzi's eye

Furthermore, the mummy can be observed far more closely and changes seen that the human eye would not normally register. We are always discovering new, interesting details such as the existence of an eyelash on the right eye.'

POPULAR INTEREST AND COMMERCIALIZATION

The Mummy as a Media Figure

Never before had an archaeological find caused as much media interest as that of the Iceman. As soon as his inconceivably old age had been made public, he started to appear on the front pages of international newspapers and magazines.

In order to deal with inquiries from the press and the international scientific community, the University of Innsbruck founded the Institute for Early Alpine History.

In contrast to other sensational archaeological finds – such as the gold treasures of Priamos or the tomb of Tutankhamun – media interest centred not on the discovery of treasure or our obsession with gold and precious stones, but on the mummified body of an unknown man in his normal clothes, carrying objects made of wood, bone, stone and copper.

 Fowler, B.: Der Mann aus dem Eis und die Rolle der Medien. In: Die Gletschermumie aus den Kupferzeit. Schriften des Südtiroler Archäologiemuseums 1. Bozen 1999, pp. 31–38.

 Fowler, B.: La mummia dei ghiacci. La storia di Ötzi cacciatore preistorico delle Alpi. Piemme 2000.

Ötzi in cartoons

Many cartoonists, some extremely well known, have long used the figure of the Iceman in their illustrations.

10 YEARS OF ÖTZI – RESURRECTION...

PURGATORY...

THIS AIN'T HOW I IMAGINED THE HEREAFTER!

„Eismann" von 4866 Jahren

Gerangel um den Bronzezeitmann

THE ICEMAN'S SECRETS

The discovery of a frozen Stone Age man yields new clues about life in 3300 B.C.

DER BOTE AUS DER STEINZEIT

Kann die Wissenschaft die Nachrichten des Similaun-Mannes dechiffrieren?

Aveva un tumore l'«uomo del ghiacciaio»

Hatte »Gletschermann« Tumor?

Forse non era solo

Il ghiaccio può nascondere ancora clamorose sorprese

„Homo Tirolensis" muß für Schaufensterdekorationen, T-Shirts und Liedtexte herhalten

Der „Ötzi" wird skrupellos vermarktet

Mummia sospetta

E se il ritrovamento sul Similaun in realtà fosse tutta una messa in scena?

Recuperati i resti mummificati dell'uomo trovato sul ghiacciaio

E' forse un guerriero dell'esercito del duca Federico «Tascavuota»

La science a reconstitué le visage de notre plus lointain ancêtre

Cet homme a 5 300 ans

On peut voir, pour la première fois, le visage de « l'homme des glaces » retrouvé en septembre 1991. **John Gurche**, à la demande de « National Geographic », a réalisé cet exploit.

»Basislager« des Gletschermannes?

Archäologen haben wegen des Wintereinbruchs Suche bis Frühjahr eingestellt

Dopo 4000 anni è finita la pace per l'uomo trovato sul ghiacciaio

Hanno fatto la Tac alla mummia

Ipotesi sulla morte: tumore cerebrale?   Forse in Italia il rinvenimento

L'Homo Tirolensis ci aiuterà a conoscere le malattie dell'antichità

Neue Einsichten vom Eismann

Ötzi wird fünf und hält die Wissenschaft auf Trab.

Souvenirs, Souvenirs

Every day, visitors from all over the world enter the South Tyrol Archaeology Museum to be fascinated, astonished and strangely moved by the sight of a witness of their past. The personal fate of one man is an emotive subject that makes history come to life. However, it is never long before an exceptional find of this kind becomes a marketable item. To exploit the fate of the Iceman, folk songs, cartoons, post cards, Ötzi jelly babies, Ötzi ice cream and Ötzi pizza all came into being and his face started to be printed on T-shirts and wine labels. The souvenir industry did not fail to take full advantage of the opportunities afforded by the Iceman.

On Stage

In September 2001, the Ötzi musical 'Frozen Fritz' opened at the Stadttheater in Bolzano.

In the Footsteps of Ötzi: Excursions

ArcheoParc Schnals (I)

The ArcheoParc Schnals is located at 1,500 m above sea level in the South Tyrolean village of Unsere Frau in Schnals. The showrooms and the adjoining areas – presenting reconstructions of various Late Stone Age buildings and research projects – illustrate the life and activities of the inhabitants of the Schnals Valley during Ötzi's lifetime. There are also educational programmes and workshops.

ArcheoParc Schnals
Unsere Frau 163
I-39020 Karthaus
Tel. 0039/0473/676020
www.archeoparc.it
info@archeoparc.it

There are numerous guided tour: to and around the site of the discovery of the Iceman

The Ötzi Show Gallery (Italy)
In the station building of the Schnals Valley glacier cable-car, there is an exhibition with displays and reconstructions of the most important details relating to the Iceman.
www.valsenales.com

Archaeological Walks
In the Schnals, Vinschgau, Passeier and Ötz Valleys, signposted archaeological walking routes on both sides of the border have been established which take in the most important archaeological sites.
Special signs indicate the routes and the sites are marked with copper posts. Information brochures displaying panoramic maps, contour lines and descriptions of the archaeological sites are available from tourist offices and shops in each of the valleys.
www.oetzisworld.it

High mountain tour to the site of the Iceman finds (Italy): tour leaves from the mountain station of the Schnals Valley glacier cable-car and goes via Hochjochferner and Schwarzwand to the Hauslabjoch at 3,279 metres. From there the walk goes up to the Tisenjoch, the place where the Iceman was discovered. Passing by the Similaun refuge, the path leads down to the Tisen Valley and finally to the town of Vernagt am See. The walk takes around seven hours.
The Passeier-Schnals Mountain Guides Association runs guided tours and supplies the necessary equipment.

Mountain Guide Association Passeier-Schnals
I-39015 St. Leonhard in Passeier
Tel. 0039/0473/656788, berge@tin.it

AUF DEN SPUREN DES MANNES AUS DEM EIS

VERNAGT - NIEDERJOCH
HAUSLABJOCH - VENT

Foto und Texte: **GIANNI BODINI**

A2

ARCHÄOLOGISCHER WANDERWEG

☞ Bodini, G.: Auf den Spuren des Mannes aus dem Eis. Schnalstal–Vinschgau–
Vent. Archäologische Wanderwege. Kulturverein Schnals 1998.

Ötzidorf in Umhausen (Austria)

'An adventure for the whole family', promises the museum/village at Umhausen in the Ötz Valley. Visitors can see the buildings constructed for Kurt Mündl's documentary film, 'The Ötz Valley Man and His World' as well as several other reconstructions.
The Tyrol Survival School offers courses where different primeval skills can be learnt.

Ötzidorf Umhausen
A-6441 Umhausen – Ötztal/Tirol
Tel. 0043/5255/50022
www.oetzidorf.at
office@oetzi-dorf.com

SELECTED BIBLIOGRAPHY AND FILMS RELATING TO THE SUBJECT

Books

Bortenschlager, Sigmar/Oeggl, Klaus (Eds.): The Iceman and his Natural Environment: Palaeobotanical Results (The Man in the Ice. Vol. 4). Wien/New York, Springer 2000.

De Marinis, Raffaele: Ötzi. La mummia del Similaun. L'uomo venuto dal ghiaccio. Venezia, Marsilio 1998.

Egg, Markus: Die Gletschermumie vom Ende der Steinzeit aus den Ötztaler Alpen. Mainz, Verlag des Römisch-Germanischen Zentralmuseums 1993.

Fowler, Brenda: La mummia dei ghiacci. La storia di Ötzi cacciatore preistorico delle Alpi. Casale Monferrato, Piemme 2000.

Fowler, Brenda: Iceman. Uncovering the Life and Times of a Prehistoric Man Found in an Alpine Glacier. New York, Random House 2000.

Goedecker-Ciolek, Roswitha: Konservierung der Beifunde einer Gletschermumie vom Ende der Steinzeit. In: Arbeitsblätter für Restauratoren 2/94. Mainz, Verlag des Römisch-Germanischen Zentralmuseums.

Höpfel, Frank et al. (Eds.): Bericht über das Internationale Symposium 1992 in Innsbruck (The Man in the Ice. Vol. 1). Innsbruck 1992.

Pedrotti, Annaluisa: L'età del Rame. In: Storia del Trentino I. La preistoria e la protostoria. Bologna, Il Mulino 2000, pp. 183–253.

Rastbichler Zissernig, Elisabeth: Der Mann im Eis. Die Fundgeschichte. Innsbruck, The innsbruck univeristy press 2006.

Rey, Françoise: Ötzi. La momie des glaciers. Grenoble, Editions Glénat 1994. Offprint from: Jahrbuch des Römisch-Germanischen Zentralmuseums Mainz 39/1992.

Spindler, Konrad: Der Mann im Eis. München, C. Bertelsmann [4]2000.

Spindler, Konrad: Der Mann im Eis. Neue sensationelle Erkenntnisse über die Mumie aus den Ötztaler Alpen. München, Goldmann 1995.

Ötzi in Folio Verlag publications

Demetz, Stefan: The South Tyrol Museum of Archaeology. The Guide. Wien/Bozen, Folio ²2000.

Fleckinger, Angelika/Steiner, Hubert: Faszination Jungsteinzeit. Der Mann aus dem Eis/Il fascino del Neolitico. L'Uomo venuto dal ghiaccio/The fascination of the Neolithic Age. The Iceman. Wien/Bozen, Folio ²2003.

Samadelli, Marco (Ed.): The Chalcolithic Mummy. In Search of Immortality. Vol. 3 (Schriften des Südtiroler Archäologiemuseums 4). Wien/Bozen, Folio 2006.

Südtiroler Archäologiemuseum (Ed.): Die Gletschermumie aus der Kupferzeit. Neue Forschungsergebnisse zum Mann aus dem Eis/La mummia dell'età del rame. Nuove ricerche sull'Uomo venuto dal ghiaccio (Schriften des Südtiroler Archäologiemuseums 1). Wien/Bozen, Folio 1999.

Sulzenbacher, Gudrun: The Glacier Mummy. Discovering the Neolithic Age with the Iceman. Wien/Bozen, Folio ²2005.

Sulzenbacher, Gudrun: Vom Büchermachen. Wie Ötzi ins Buch kam. Wien/Bozen, Folio 2005.

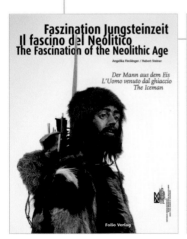

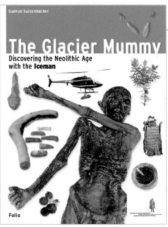

Spindler, Konrad: L'Uomo dei ghiacci. Confine italo-austriaco: la scoperta di un corpo di cinquemila anni fa rivela i segreti dell'età della pietra. Milano, Nuova Pratiche Editrice 1998.

Spindler, Konrad et al. (Eds.): Der Mann im Eis. Neue Funde und Ergebnisse (The Man in the Ice. Vol. 2). Wien/New York, Springer 1995.

Spindler, Konrad: The Man in the Ice. The discovery of a 5.000 Year Old Body Reveals the Secrets of the Stone Age. New York, Harmony Books 1994.

Spindler, Konrad et al. (Eds.): Human Mummies: A Global Survey of their Status and the Techniques of Conservation (The Man in the Ice. Vol. 3). Wien/New York, Springer 1996.

Films

Death of the Iceman. BBC – British Broadcasting Corporation, UK – London.

Der Mann aus dem Eis. Wie Wissenschaftler aus aller Welt das Geheimnis der 5300 Jahre alten Gletschermumie Ötzi lüften. VHS, Spiegel TV, 97 minutes.

Der Ötztal-Mann und seine Welt. Das Jahr bevor er schlief. VHS, Movienet Film GmbH, 93 minutes.

Iceman: Hunt for a Killer. Discovery Communications Incorporated, USA/Brando Quilici Productions, Italy.

'Ötzi' – Der Mann aus dem Eis. VHS, FWU – Wissen und Bildung, 27 minutes

Ultimate Guide, Iceman. Discovery Communications Incorporated, USA/Brando Quilici Productions, Italy.

GLOSSARY

Adipocere: Also known as grave wax or mortuary fat, adipocere describes the transformation of body fat into a fatty, soapy substance on the surface of corpses, particularly those which have lain in ice for a long time.

Australopithecus: Term for various primates who lived 3.5 million years ago and represent the link between the apes and Homo sapiens, characterized by walking upright

Glacier corpses often show signs of adipocere.

Beau-Reil Cross Furrows: Furrows appearing across the nails after serious infection or poisoning resulting from an interruption in nail growth

Cross-stitching: sewing technique in which lacing together makes the edge appear serrated

Decontamination room: Room for carrying out disinfection processes

Dehydration: Loss or deprivation of water

Diastema: Gap between two teeth, particularly between the upper central incisors

Ectoparasites: Parasites living off the body surface

Endoparasites: Parasites living inside the body

Epidermis: Blood vessel free, outer cell layer of the skin

Flint: Stone which, on account of its sharp, shell-like structure, is used in the building of weapons and objects and in making fire.

Histology: Study of body tissue, its structure and particular qualities

Isotopes: Atoms; almost all chemical elements are mixtures of isotopes

Juanita: Name given to the mummy of a 14-year-old Inca girl found on the slopes of the Ampato volcano in the Peruvian Andes. The dry, icy climate preserved the mummy for over 500 years.

Lindow Man: Name given to the 2,300-year-old marsh corpse discovered in Cheshire, UK, in 1984. Today it is on display in the British Museum in London.

Mitochondrial DNA: Mitochondrials are thread-like or spherical structures found in human, animal and plant cells which support the breathing and the metabolism of the cells. All mitochondrials contain a ring-shaped DNA.

Osteone: Element of bone tissue

Paleoclimatic data: Data on the climatic development of primeval times

Physiognomy: Individual expression of a face

Prune: To rid trees of superfluous branches and shoots

Radial fletching: Flight path stabiliser at the end of an arrow, usually made of feathers and usually three-fold

Situla: Bronze conical cult container engraved with images

Stonehenge: Megalithic site dating back to the 3rd or 2nd millennium BC north of Salisbury in South England

Sublimation: Direct transformation from a solid to a gaseous aggregate state

Technical archaeologist: Experts who recreate ancient techniques experimentally. Using archaeological finds as archetypes, they elaborate new objects or tools and check their effectiveness.

Tisenjoch: Crossing over the main Alpine ridge linking the Schnals and Ötz valleys

Tollund Man: A very well preserved moor corpse, dating back to the time around the birth of Christ, was found on Tollund Moor in 1950 in Denmark.

Typology: Science of attributing to groups on the basis of a comprehensive set of characteristics which characterise human-beings

Reconstruction of an arrow using feathers of the common buzzard

t = top
b = bottom
r = right
m = middle
l = left

PICTURE CREDITS

Amt für Bodendenkmäler der
 Autonomen Provinz Bozen-
 Südtirol: pp. 26, 30, 28–29 b
Angelantoni, Cesare: p. 104
Archeoparc Schnals: p. 111 t/b
Bundeskriminalamt Wiesbaden
 (K. Kramer): p. 33 m
Capasso, Luigi, Museo Archeologico
 Nazionale, Chieti: p. 37
Discovery Chanel: p. 105
Folio Verlag: p. 116
• no.parking: pp. 21, 25 r, 48, 85 b,
 89 t
• Seehauser, Othmar: p. 25 l
• Sulzenbacher, Gudrun: p. 24
Galler, Stefan, Universität Salzburg:
 p. 40
GEO 10/1996, p. 74 f.: pp. 34–35
Gothe, Rainer/Schöl, Heidrun,
 München: p. 33 b
Greenland National Museum, Nuuk:
 p. 52
Hanny, Paul, Grammy Liasion: p. 49
Kulturverein Schnals: p. 113
Landesgendarmeriekommando für
 Tirol: pp. 11, 16 t, 29 tl, 70
Mapgraphic: panoramic map inside
 front cover
Musei civici di Reggio Emilia (Virgilio
 Artioli): p. 92 t
Nosko, Werner: p. 17
Oportot, Mónica, National Museum
 of Natural History, Chile: p. 54
Ötzidorf Umhausen: p. 114
Paulsen, Harm: pp. 43 t, 79 l/r, 84
Quilici, Brando: p. 30
Reinhard, Johan: p. 22
Rolle, Renate, Hamburg (after
 Artamonov): p. 42 t
Römisch-Germanisches Zentral-
 museum Mainz: pp. 57, 58, 75 t,
 76 tm/r

Silkeborg Museum, Hovedgaarden,
 Silkeborg: p. 53
South Tyrol Museum of Archaeology:
 pp. 50, 47
• Gruppe Gut: pp. 42 b, 68 t/b, 69,
 71, 91
• Ochsenreiter, Augustin: cover
 photograph, pp. 20, 28 l/r, 29
 bl/br, 29 tr, 31, 38 t/b, 41, 43 b,
 51 t/b, 56, 59, 60, 61, 62 t, 63,
 64, 65 t/b, 66, 72 b, 73, 74, 75 b,
 76 tl/b, 77, 78 t/b, 80, 81 l/r, 82,
 83 t, 83 bl/m/r, 85 t/m, 86, 87 t,
 87 bl/m/r, 88, 89 t, 90, 92 b, 96,
 98 tl/r, 98 b, 99, 102–103, 107 t,
 110 t, 119
• Pernter, Josef: pp. 100, 106
• Putzer, Johanna und Katherina:
 drawings in the timeline
• Samadelli, Marco: pp. 23, 44, 46,
 97, 107 b
• Seehauser, Othmar: pp. 9, 14, 94,
 101 t/b
• Welponer, Sara: pp. 3, 62 b, cover
 drawings
Stadttheater Bozen: p. 110 b
Tappeiner Werbefoto & Verlag:
 pp. 8–9
Tischler, Peppi: p. 108
Universität Innsbruck: pp. 12, 16 b,
 32, 39 b, 118
• Maurer, Helmuth: p. 39 t
• Oeggl, Klaus: p. 50 b
• Sommer, Gerhard: p. 72 tl/m/r
• zur Nedden, Dieter: pp. 36 t/b, 45
University of Alberta (Owen Beattie):
 p. 54 t
Uno Press: p. 13 t/b
Vienna Report: pp. 15, 18, 67